The Heat of the Night

by

Elissa Gabrielle, Niyah Moore, LaLaina Knowles,
Lorraine Elzia, Pynk, Ebonee Monique

Giving Your Soul a Rise...One Page at a Time

ISBN-13: 978-0-9850763-1-3

Peace In The Storm Publishing, LLC.
P.O. Box 1152
Pocono Summit, PA 18346
www.peaceinthestormpublishing.com
www.theheatofthenight.net

The Heat of the Night

by

*Elissa Gabrielle, Niyah Moore, LaLaina Knowles,
Lorraine Elzia, Pynk, Ebonee Monique*

The captivating allure of a woman is magnetic to all she encounters. Her aura is defined by intrigue and passion. She possesses the power to enchant, seduce and conquer at will with her heart, her mind, her body and her words. Warm as the sun, dipped in ebony majesty, she is full in rhythm and complete notes; harmonious, fluid, sexy. She is never to be underestimated for she has the ability to transform galaxies and move continents from the sizzling kiss of her lips. From the pen of six femme fatales, comes a sweltering journey in erotic pleasure and adventure. This collection of steamy escapades is a savory blend of sensual encounters that revel in lust, obsession, and uncontrollable desire. Take a walk on the wild side as fantasy begins from the sultry moans uttered from lovers' lips. Insatiable attractions and deep desires materialize through sizzling prose guaranteed to ignite a fire within which is experienced only in The Heat of the Night.

The Heat of the Night features some of the most-talented authors in the game. Sizzling stories by Pynk, Elissa Gabrielle, Lorraine Elzia, Ebonee Monique, LaLaina Knowles and Niyah Moore, empowering women to take charge of their climax... one page at a time.

Praise for
The Heat of the Night

"Elissa Gabrielle is definitely a force to be reckoned with. She is the gift that keeps on giving. Deliciously delectable, sensually seductive and poetically pervasive; she deliberately delivers the heat from start to finish. Her words promise to have you fanning yourself as sweat drips from your forehead. Without a doubt, I'm officially on Team Elissa."

~ *Rory D. Sheriff, Radio Personality and Best Selling Author of Get'n Serious*

"Singeing the pages with heat, PYNK finds the center of the Triangle and hits it repeatedly. Arousing you with every word, by the end of this journey you'll fight orgasmic tremors, then ask for a cigarette. Some good stuff right here..."

~ *William Fredrick Cooper, Award-winning Essence Bestselling Author of There's Always a Reason*

"You are not ready for what LaLaina Knowles has in store with "Far Way" - plain and simple! Constance inadvertently turns a message from her long-lost friend, Trey, into an affinity that's equal parts affection and appetite. Sparks fly when they meet up. But is it just a part of two? This fraction of fiction is a fiery flame that will burn the paper and will melt the screen of your favorite ebook reader. Witness a scorching desire that 20 years could not extinguish."

~ *Joey Pinkney, Author, Book Reviewer, Contributor to The Soul of a Man*

"When temperature are set to it's highest degree anything can happen for lethal to be legit -- Niyah Moore's 'Lethally Yours' is more for your reading pleasure!"

~ *Alvin C. Romer, The Romer Review*

"Ebonee brings pure fire with her lustful writing style and passionate spin on eroticism."

~ *Torrian Ferguson, ESSENCE Best-Selling Author*

"When fire, sweat, and steam congregate, you can bet the meeting place is right in the middle of a Lorraine Elzia story. In 'Le Boudoir', the thermostat lever is moved all the way to the right...and stays there."

~ *Marc Lacy, Author and Poet*

Triangle
By
Pynk

Prologue
September 18, 2011

Naked.

I had shed my black satin bra and panties and tossed them on the white tile floor.

My panties were laced with the scent of lust.

It was just after midnight.

The oval jetted tub for two contained only one.

The flickering candlelight added to the seduction.

I just couldn't resist touching myself.

The sweet scent of the black-cherry bubble bath filled the master bathroom. My surrendering body soaked in the lap of luxury, from the tip of my rosy red toes to the crack of my round behind, and up the width of my back to the top of my shoulder blades. I leaned against the tub. The pulsating jets hit all the right places. Every single one of them.

My hands were lost beneath the sudsy water. Suds that hid the sight of my self-pleasure. I was on fire while my husband of ten years slept just outside the door.

I touched myself with fingers that probed beneath hot water that was no match for the heat seeping from between my legs. Slow-moving steam arose from the water's surface, slowly seeping into my skin, causing my face to sweat, giving off a warm mist, saturating my hair that was pulled back into a bun.

I opened my legs to explore myself more. More finger-fucking. More solo-love. More masturbating. My fingers knew me well.

My one hand rubbed along the soft womanly design of my full, slippery lips. Surrendering lips that guarded the entry to my vagina, framing my womanhood. My middle finger had already found its way inside—and then my index finger, and then my ring finger—probing my walls with curiosity as if my wish was their command.

My only wish was for an underwater orgasm created by the unbridled fantasy in my head. The vision of the one we met earlier that evening. My thoughts were extreme.

My thoughts were of her.

It was a Sunday and my husband Marcel and I would usually go watch football somewhere. I went along just to be with him. We live near Dallas, Texas and he's a Dallas Cowboys fanatic. I can take it or leave it actually. But I watched the game with him because he asked me to. I enjoyed pleasing my husband. Something my mother never did for my dad.

My runway model friend named Piper Owens was dating a new guy named Tyrone. He was a chocolate, bald, track runner whose voice said he was country as a dozen eggs. He spoke like he was hung like Mandingo. Knowing Piper's style, he also had a little money. She invited us to his house in Richardson, Texas which was eleven miles from our house in

Plano. His place was new, large, and filled with people.

After about an hour into being there, a woman walked in. I saw Marcel look at her. Most of the men did. But, what I also noticed was that she looked at me. I turned back toward the view of the game, trying not to stare, but she didn't try not to at all. I took in her sight and gave a smile. She smiled more. I looked away. I looked back. She was still smiling.

She wore the hell out of her dark stonewash jeans. The tight white top she wore showed off how she was drawn. Her big bust and tiny waist. Her burgundy pixie haircut framed her toffee face. Her facial structure was perfection; cheekbones classic.

Tyrone didn't bother to introduce anybody. The woman went out into the backyard with Piper. I stayed on the couch next to Marcel. A few guys shook their heads at the view of her from behind. One said, "Damn!" Marcel watched football; drinking a beer.

A while later, I'd gone from the living room, down the hall, looking inside of one room, hoping it was the bathroom but it wasn't. I went back down the hall to a different door and opened it. Jackpot. Just as I stepped one foot inside, a sultry voice behind me said, "Oh. Sorry. You beat me to it."

I turned back and looked up. It was her. Blue jean wearing, fine ass, her. My hand was along the doorknob, and she placed her hand on top of mine. Her hand was soft. And it was hot. She didn't move hers. I didn't move mine. I brought my eyes to hers.

"Sorry. You can go first." I took in her scent. It was sweet pineapple.

She gave me a sweet look. "No. I'll wait. You go first." Her snow white teeth were exposed.

"Okay." But I still looked at her as she still kept her hand on mine. Flirting. It seemed like ten minutes. Actually, it seemed like an hour. I eyed her chest. Her deep cleavage was visible. I'd guess 38F. Her coffee-brown breasts touched each other. They were full.

She looked at my lips, then my chin, then my chest, then below my waist with a look that said, I would if you'd let me.

Surely my blushed face asked, What? Lick me. My mouth said, "I'll be right out."

I made myself turn. She removed her hand, immediately tapping my backside with the sound of a Pop.

If it was a man who had slapped my ass, I would've slapped him dead in his face.

But what I did instead was look back with approval. My pussy cosigned.

I closed the door. My body melted against it. I forgot what I'd come in there for in the first place. My nipples were erect. My vagina was wet. My panties were moist.

Before long, Marcel and I left Tyrone's place and went home; but she lingered in my head. Undeniably, she had awakened something inside me.

As I continued to bathe, my hand moved up to my nipple, my thumb flicking. I cupped my entire breast, squeezing myself like it belonged to her; finger inside of myself like my insides were hers.

My fingers then found their way back to my clit. They pressed, rubbed, flicked. I clenched my pussy around my fingers. She was in my head. Her titties, her eyes, her touch, her hand along my ass. I had a fantasy-filled vision of me on my back with her face between my legs, licking, doing what her eyes told me her mouth would do. Her hips in the air, and Marcel standing behind her. His dick plunging in and out of her creamy vagina. Him getting some pussy, her getting some dick and me getting some head. All of us intertwined in a threesome paradise.

I closed my legs, feeling my walls throb to the x-rated sight in my mind. My outer lips contracted while my left hand brought my clit to its peak, rubbing it furiously as it expanded, escorting my escaping orgasm that released itself with a fury into the water. It tightened and released again. And again. My heart raced with excitement and my breathing sped up. I fought to tame my private thrill and moaned, "Uhhhhhhhhhhh." It sounded like I was crying quietly. I waited, riding it through.

I patted my pussy and rested my head back upon the tub. That was so real. So vivid. So hot.

I'm not like most women. For ten years I've fanaticized about my husband fucking a woman while I watched. Any woman. But tonight it was him fucking her in my mind. If only I could take it from my head to the bed so that my fantasies could become reality. Then I could finally see my husband of ten years pleasing another woman.

A woman for him. Marcel Cooper.

A woman for me. Mona Cooper.

I'd gone there twenty years ago without him.

And I was so ready to finally go there again with him.

My curiosity itched again.

And this time, I just had to scratch it.

I refused to be just like my uptight mother.

Chapter One

It was almost three weeks later, early afternoon on a Thursday. Mona Cooper arrived back from lunch to her job as manager of the Bath and Body Works in the Galleria Mall in Dallas. It was a seventy-degree day, in spite of it being October. Mona had just clocked back in on one of the cash registers when she walked in.

She was tall and curvy, thick, like she was cornbread fed and country raised; yet strong, like an athlete. She wore a burgundy, healthy looking precision haircut. Those classic cheekbones.

Mona's eye were stuck. Her feet were cemented to the floor. Her chest pounded.

There she was again, walking toward the register with her sturdy, sexy stroll, looking Mona straight in the eyes with a big smile. She stopped before her, smelling like pineapple.

The woman spoke first. Her teeth were pearly white.

"How are you? Good to see you again."

"I'm good, and you?" Mona smiled back.

"I'm better now."

"Good. Good." Dang, she's really good. "Just getting back from lunch."

"I see."

Mona crossed her arms, tapped her foot. Breathed. "So my timing is pretty good then, huh?"

"I'd say so." The woman looked Mona down more than up.

"What'd you have?"

"Chinese."

"Love Chinese." The woman gave a smile and handed Mona the two items; coconut pineapple shower gel and sweet pea body lotion.

Mona stepped behind the counter to the register, adding a little more of a switch than usual.

The woman noticed and asked, "So, how do you know Piper and Tyrone."

"Oh, we—my husband and I—don't know Tyrone," Mona replied. "But Piper worked here last year. She's my friend. We don't know each other that well, be we talk when we can."

"I see. I met Piper where I work. She's cool people."

"Yes, she is." Mona scanned the two items, ringing them up. "Will that be it for you?"

"For now." She asked, eyeing Mona down, "Anyone ever tell you, you look like Alicia Keys?"

"A couple of times. Yeah." Mona nodded.

"You do." She gave sexy eyes. "You are fine as fuck."

Mona gave a quick laugh, checking to see if her coworker was within earshot. "Well, thanks. So are you." She blushed.

"Thanks." The woman slid her credit card through the card reader and signed her name along the screen.

"Okay. Here you go," Mona said, handing her the bag. "So what is it that you do?"

The woman took the bag and at the same time handed Mona her business card. "Here. How about giving me a call and I'll tell you all about it?"

Mona smiled inside and gave an internal sigh of relief. "Okay." She read the card. "I'll do that, Athena Rowland. Pretty name."

"Thanks. And you are?"

She felt a little nervous. "I'm Mona. I'm the manger."

"Okay Mona, the manger." Athena leaned closer. "Now don't forget to call. I don't want to go to bed tonight realizing I haven't heard from you."

Mona looked certain, nodding. "Oh, I'll call."

"I hope so. See you later. Or should I say sooner."

"Sooner." Mona looked at her like she was way too smooth.

An associate walked back behind the counter, Athena said coyly, "Thank you," and she stepped away toward the door.

Mona replied to her back, taking a visual snapshot of every inch of the contour of Athena's plump behind. "Thank you for shopping at Bath and Body Works."

The sight of it made Mona's girlie nature rise.

Chapter Two

That same evening, by eleven-thirty, it was Mona and her husband Marcel in their master suite of their four-bedroom home in the Estates of Russell Creek.

He laid on his back with his head at the foot of their king bed. Mona stood next to the bed nude—facing away from his body, straddling him so her pussy was directly on his face, his hands along her supple ass-cheeks. His dark skin against her light skin. Their tones were opposites. Their souls were not.

The ambiance of the fireplace was aglow.

The sweet essence of the hot-buttered rum diffuser filled the air.

He was at full attention below his waist even though he focused on pleasing her.

He sniffed her sweaty estrogen scent, pointed his tongue and licked the outside of her juiced-up vagina, then flattened his tongue along her soft lips. He then worked his way to her opening; separating her labia beneath her coils of curly hair as he moved his mouth up to her clitoris. He gave her his signature move of flicking it, giving fast motions like a butterfly; the move that not only made Mona come, but if it was a really good one, she would sometimes sound as if she was crying.

Her imagination was on extra-high, just as it had been for a few weeks now. She looked down at his handsome face and her excitement grew. She took in the sight of him wearing the pussy mustache of her trimmed vagina. In her mind she saw Athena sitting on his face in her place. She wondered if Athena was also unshaven, just the way her man liked. "Ahhh." She sucked her teeth and gave a moan like a sex queen, holding her breasts in her hands.

"Yes. Oh yes. Ummh, shit. Shit. Baby wait. Not yet." She tried to step away, one hand on his curly head and one on his buffed shoulder.

He kept at it, holding on to her thighs, forbidding her departure. His muscular arms flexed.

She spilled the words that had been in her head for days now. "Baby, I met someone today. She's so fucking fine. I promise you."

He still kept at it.

"I want us to get with her. You and me."

He stopped, pushing her hips upward. He licked his lips. She stood and turned toward him.

"What are you talking about?"

She took a deep breath and just let it all out. "I've wanted to talk to you about this. Honestly, I keep thinking about her in my head when we have sex. Baby, I want her to feel what you do to me."

"Her who? Who are you talking about?"

She sat on the edge of the bed next to his fit body. "This girl I met today at work. Actually, she's the same girl who came by Tyrone's house when we were there last month watching the game. She knows Piper. Her name is Athena. She's the one who walked in and the whole party stopped. The one with the short haircut and the body that everyone couldn't stop staring at. I know you remember her."

He stared at her and paused, then said, "I do."

"Do you think she's sexy?" Mona scooted closer to him.

He looked reserved but said anyway, "Yes. Yes, I do. I won't lie. But Mona, our thing is we look without being disrespectful to each other. We don't touch. Never have."

"She gave me her number."

He looked confused. "When? That day? Or at the store?"

"At the store today."

"And you called her?"

"I did. It's time to touch."

He shook his head, looking away and then back to her. "Damn, Mona."

"Baby listen. After all these years, I'm not trying to mess our thing up, but you know I had a threesome in college. Quentin and I got with that white chick I told you about. The three of us did it a few times."

"Yes. But that was a long time ago. Why bring this up now?"

"We've talked about threesomes before."

"We have. As a fantasy."

"I know. And I know you never had one."

"I haven't. And as far as I'm concerned, I won't." He scooted all the way back to the headboard and adjusted the pillow behind himself.

"But why not?"

"Why would we is the question? For me, I just can't have my wife watching me please someone else." He looked at her. "That's cheating, plain and simple. Even if you are in the room."

"Honestly, I think watching would turn me the hell on."

He shook his head. "I don't think so."

"So you don't think you could let go enough to just enjoy yourself? To live out the fantasy."

"I think that if she even began to please me, I doubt I could relax enough to enjoy it. If you ask me, I say we leave well enough alone."

"Marcel, come on. This is every man's fantasy. You mean to tell me you wouldn't at least give it a try?"

"First of all it, it's not my fantasy. That's my concern; because it's your fantasy and not mine. Some people are smart enough to not go there."

"Please."

He looked at her like he didn't even know her anymore. Her words were so different after a decade of marriage. "I can't believe it's almost like you're begging me."

"I am. I want to do it. But, I won't do it without you."

He gave a heavy sigh. "Who is she, anyway? You've talked to her?"

"I did. She works as a lap dance instructor near the mall. She came in to buy her regular items, but I'd never seen her before we were at Tyrone's house. She said she wanted to take me out to dinner. She knows you're my husband and that I wouldn't do anything behind your back. She told me you were handsome and that she noticed you sitting on the couch when she first stepped in. She's the one who then said to me, 'let's do it in front of him.' She asked if you'd be down."

He looked both flattered and reserved. "It's like that?"

"It is. She's ready. I'm ready."

Mona stood up and then got on all fours, crawling like

Catwoman between Marcel's long legs. His wide dick had subsided a few minutes earlier, but was now standing straight up. She bent down to it, licking it. It jumped, cooperating with her though he seemed not to want to.

He just looked down at her. "You have lost your mind. How could you handle seeing me with someone else?"

She talked close to the tip of his dick. "I don't want you to be in love with another woman, I just want you to have sex with her in front of me."

"Really?" The look on his face told that the whole conversation was unbelievable to him. "And you want her to be with you too?"

"I do."

"What does that have to do with me?"

Mona looked up and gave a seductive look. "I want you to watch me eat pussy. I'm pretty good at it. It's said to be like riding a bike. You never forget." She kissed his scrotum.

"You doing that is not something I need to see."

"But do you want to see it? Do you want to watch me make her come with my mouth? That's the question." She began sucking him.

He just watched.

She spit on his dick and smeared the saliva up and down the length of his shaft, from his testicles to his head. She sucked deeper, twisting her left hand to guide him all the way inside. Her deep throat skills were his most major turn on.

He rested his head back.

She released him from her mouth and said, "And I want to watch her fuck you while I kiss you." She resumed.

He grunted as she went down further, seeming to give in to the imagination behind his closed eyes.

She took him fully into her mouth, like she could chew

him up and swallow him; like it would be her pleasure for him to fit down her throat. She moved up and down his shaft, circling his head with her tongue, holding him deep inside as far as she could until she was in danger of losing her breath, and then sliding her lips back up to his dark, mushroom-shaped head. The sound of her slobbery blow-job was messy.

He gave a deep breath, quickly looking down at her again and sounded restless. "I'm about to . . ."

"Uh-huh." She gave a tighter grip and maintained pressure, moving up and down his length faster, using precise sucking movements while his shaft widened even more. It expanded against her hand.

"Fuck," he said, flexing every muscle in his body while he shot fast-moving streams of semen in her mouth. She swallowed twice and released him from her mouth, licking his tip as remnant drops escaped.

She said in a sex-kitten voice, "That was from Athena. She told me to suck it just like that." She stood, heading for the bathroom.

"Damn, baby." He breathed deep and looked at his dick that wouldn't go down. He said loudly in her direction, "Hook it up."

She replied with pleasure, "That a boy. I love you."

"I love you, too."

Chapter Three

It was the next day.

A Friday.

Having kinky, out-of-the-box thoughts in her head all day at work, Mona called Athena as soon as her shift was done. She pulled off in her blue Maxima, first stopping by the grocery store.

After their mutual greetings, Mona told her with a playful tone, "I'm calling your bluff."

"What bluff, boo?"

"About what you said. You said, 'let's do it in front of him.' In front of my husband."

"Yep. I did."

"Then let's. My husband said for me to hook it up."

Athena's reply was swift. "I'm game."

"Cool." A few nervous seconds went by. "Yep. That'll be good. So let me ask you this...are you into dudes; like do you date men?"

"I do. I had someone for about three years. We broke up a few months ago."

"Okay. And women? When did that start?"

"Well, I can tell you one thing, I wasn't born that way. It happened when I was in high school. I was a stripper. I looked twenty-two, but I was only seventeen. I'm actually thirty now."

"Really?"

"Yep. I've always looked older. One of the girls and I fooled around for about a year. It's not like I look for ladies. But every now and then someone catches my eye. Like when I saw you. You just...I don't know. I was just attracted."

"I could definitely tell that. In my case, I haven't acted on it in twenty years."

"Wow. Why now?"

"Something about you. Like you said, 'it's an attraction.' And, I guess I'm just curious," Mona admitted.

"Well, I'm flattered." She giggled. "So, I guess you and your husband have never done this before. Or was he the one you did it with twenty years ago?"

"No. That was someone else. This time with my husband would be our first time together. But, he knows this is something I want. He says he can handle it. I'm ready. Just making sure you're down for the dick and not just him watching. Making sure that would be okay with you."

"I'm good. Done that before. Been to Club Iniquity in Dallas. I even tried the orgy room. I'm no prude. You been there before?"

"No. Heard it was cool though. Not sure my husband would go. I guess I'd have to ask."

"Yeah. It's not for everybody."

"No. So, you been tested lately?" Mona asked, taking the off-ramp toward the store.

"I have. How about you two?"

"Being married for so long...No."

"I understand."

"But we will. I know a place. You show us yours, we'll show you ours."

Athena giggled again. "That'll work. So, what's your husband's name?"

"Marcel."

"Okay. You and Marcel have any kids?"

"No. I had two miscarriages. It was tough, but we hadn't planned to have children so he had a vasectomy years ago. You have any?"

"I have an eight-year-old daughter. Years ago, I had trouble caring for her. We were living in a shelter for a while. My mom's had her for six months, but I should be able to get her soon. She just has her until I get on my feet. Things are tough."

"Yep—for a lot of people. Marcel works as an account executive for DirecTV, which means he's in sales. Commission only. And my job is cool, but I don't make as much as I thought I would at thirty-eight. Still, we work things out."

"I understand."

"And obviously we're older than you."

"Please. You look good. With your Alicia Keys ass."

This time Mona giggled. "Well, thanks." She pulled into a parking spot. "Listen, I'm at the store now, about to go inside. How about if we get together next week? On Monday maybe. My husband and I should be able to get tested by then."

"That's cool. About eight? I teach a class until six. That'll give me time to go home and get ready. I'm in Dallas."

"That'll work. We're in Plano. Can you come by our place?" Mona asked, stepping out of her car.

"I can."

"Good. I'll text you the address. I'm excited."

"Me too, boo. Talk to you later," Athena said.

"Have a good evening."

Chapter Four

It was a little after ten o'clock on Monday night.

An evening of laughter, and hours of conversation had gone by; bonding three curious adults. Actually, two were more curious than one.

The test results were all negative. The light was green.

It was time to break the rules of fidelity.

But it was also important to make sure everyone knew to follow the threesome rules of no Marcel and Athena kissing, no Marcel and Athena anal sex, and no Marcel and Athena sex on the side. It had to be right up front.

Two almost empty glasses of pink Moscato and one half-full bottle of Corona with lime sat before them.

A total of three glasses of wine each. A total of two bottles of beer.

Mona made honey salmon and yellow rice with a spinach salad. Athena had seconds. Marcel barely finished his meal.

The plates were still on the dining room table in front of them.

Marcel Cooper swallowed a swig from his beer, watching the two ladies before him; his wife, Mona, and her new friend. Both were ready, willing, and able to get it on with him, but he couldn't help but to wonder . . .what would make a woman want to share her husband with another woman, and stay in the room to watch it go down? Why would a threesome be more appealing to his wife than the intimacy of a twosome? He knew that the lifestyle of being a triple had to be more complicated than that of a couple. He wondered if two lovers could really be better than one. After all, what man doesn't want to be with two women, so why was he even thinking with his upper head as opposed to his lower? Would it be better to leave their vanilla way of living as it was and not bed down their potential mistress? Could there be such a thing as a tri-match made in heaven? Would that mean it would be three times the fun? A kinky love triangle sat down before him with the intention of spicing up a husband and wife's marriage. He and Mona were about to unzip ecstasy. Or...he wondered... would they unzip hell?

Just then, Athena stood from the table and took Marcel's wife by the hand. Mona stood and took Marcel by the hand. He stood and followed them up the stairs to the master bedroom as planned. Yes, his brain was loud, but also, he had a full-on erection showing from beneath his gray sweatpants. His dick told him to man the fuck up!

Mona and Marcel's bedroom suite had a large sitting area that was big enough for a sofa and a loveseat. It was set up like a little den, with a coffee table and a huge plasma T.V.

The amber lights were sexy. Sugar cookie candles were burning. Even the mood-setting CD was playing, "Secret Garden" by Quincy Jones.

Already, within one minute of entering the bedroom,

Mona and Athena both giggling and hugging, had managed to fall onto the king bed, barefoot but fully clothed; Mona on top. They began kissing, full tongue, eyes closed; serious.

Mona broke it off with a smack and brought her kisses down to Athena's neck. "I love the way you smell." She licked Athena's skin and sucked on her ear lobe, sticking her tongue deep inside.

Athena's eyes looked weak.

In the garden, the temptation feels so right. The music was their escort.

Marcel just watched. His face was blank.

Mona's hands were all over Athena's huge breasts. The breasts she'd fanaticized about for days.

Mona said, "Tittie girl."

Athena's hands were all over Mona's massive ass, squeezing her cheeks which were covered by tight jeans. "Ass girl. I'm gonna need you to take these off."

Mona smiled and stood, unzipping her pants. She looked over at Marcel who had made his way over to the gold loveseat, taking it all in, getting in his first sight of his wife enjoying someone other than him. She said to him with inviting eyes, "Baby, can you come help me please?"

He stood and stepped to her.

She looked at his crotch, saying to Athena, "My man is hung girl. He's got the good dick." Mona's words were slurred.

"I noticed." Athena removed her pants and top.

Mona stepped out of her pants with Marcel's help, exposing her silk panties. She took off her tee-shirt. She was braless. Her tawny nipples were pointed toward Athena who lay on her back wearing a white lace bra and thong. She had thick legs, breasts for days, and wide, child-bearing hips.

Mona said to Marcel sweetly, "Take your pants off honey.

Let Athena see what my baby's working with."

Marcel moved in slow motion, removing his pants and underwear. His dick was toffee brown, stiff, long, and wide, with a slight curve at the tip.

Mona removed his black golf shirt for him and then laid her body down upon Athena's again, sliding girlie skin upon girlie skin. "Your legs are so soft. So smooth," she said.

She inched Athena's thong down and finally completely off, and began licking her belly button, making a trail down to Athena's vulva.

Athena opened her legs and looked over at Marcel, gazing at his defined chest.

His curious eyes expanded, seeing that her large vagina was shaven. It was the color of cinnamon. The head of her long clit peeked from beyond her labia without the need of even pulling back the hood. She reached out her hand toward him but he didn't respond. It wasn't her permission that he was waiting for. He just stood over the two of them and visually took it all in.

Mona scooted Athena's hips closer and moaned at the up-close sight.

"Yummy." She began kissing her sugar thighs and sucking Athena's pussy meat and kissing her vulva, inhaling Athena's smooth, fruity smelling skin.

Athena sighed, focusing on Mona's techniques.

Mona pointed her tongue, stroking Athena's clit aggressively. The inverted V-shaped clitoris swelled in Mona's mouth.

Marcel looked very surprised.

Athena sighed. "Oh, yeah. Damn."

Mona closed her lips around Athena's clit and sucked its entirety into her mouth. She tickled it with her tongue while slurping on it. It was a lashing that made Athena squirm. Mona's arms were locked along the back of her thighs.

Marcel suddenly grabbed the width of his penis, stroking himself with his right hand while watching his wife eat a woman's pussy.

Mona used a rolling motion of her tongue while sucking Athena's clit like it was a large nipple.

Athena sounded like a lioness. "Damn. That shit feels good. I'm gonna come. Dammit." Her voice of warning was unstable.

Mona continued to suck Athena's erect clit with an airtight grip; flicking and swirling her tongue around its axis. She looked up at Athena whose eyes were shut. Her face seemed to fight to savor the ecstasy. Mona saw that as a challenge. She bobbed her head up and down like she was sucking a long dick.

Athena looked down at Mona and let out a rolling moan like a car engine about to kick over. "Yes. Yes. Oh, damn. Oooooooooh, yeah. Yeah. Oh, Monaaaaaaaaaaa!" Athena let it out and spewed her orgasm in Mona's face. Mona stayed put and rode it through until it subsided, feeling Athena's throbbing clit repeatedly burst against her tongue.

Marcel had ceased his stroking and stood even closer to them. "Damn is right."

Mona came to a stance and gave a big grin toward Athena who lay back, breathing unsteadily, sticking her finger inside of herself. "Damn, I'm wet. Holy shit."

Mona stood next to Marcel. "Come on baby. Your turn."

She took him by the hand and they both got on the bed. "You lay between us," she told him. He obeyed her order and got on his back.

Athena undid her bra. Her boobs spilled out of the cups.

She had a small Playboy tattoo over her heart.

Mona reached over and put Marcel's hand on Athena's breast.

"It's okay. You can touch her."

Marcel's fingertips caressed their fullness, moving them to make them shake. They were different from Mona's—larger, heavier, softer. He squeezed. And squeezed.

Athena asked him, as if it was casual, "Can I fuck you?"

"Yes." He then looked at Mona.

She gave permission with her smile.

Mona reached over and took the Magnum condom package from the oak nightstand and opened it, placing it on her husband's massive hardness.

Once Athena scooted over, Marcel lay on his back in her place. She adjusted herself to straddle him, leaning down to allow her hanging breasts to lie along his skin. He took one into his mouth and sucked. Athena reached back and grabbed his dick from behind her ass.

"Your dick is so big. This is gonna be the shit!"

Mona's hand began guiding Marcel's penis to Athena's opening.

With strong legs, Athena literally squatted over him like she was a gymnast, allowing his penis entry into her vagina. The first inch made him moan. It also made her moan in unison as well. She took it in more and more until it was completely inside of her, accommodating all of him. She was deep and she was wet.

She said in an erotic voice as she bounced, "This wide dick hits all the right spots. My pussy is full. Damn, Mona. You're a lucky ass girl."

Mona began kissing Marcel's lips, keeping one hand on Athena's thigh, feeling Athena's movement as she rode her husband. His dick inside of her while she watched. She was not surprised by Athena's reaction to how good it felt. She knew very well what her husband's dick could do. "Damn, that shit looks good," Mona said as she suddenly got up and backed away, leaving them to each other.

For a second, Marcel watched her get further away, but the more Athena bucked her ass against his balls, fucking him like an adult film star, the more Marcel looked away from his wife and concentrated on the woman he was dicking-down.

Athena placed his hands on her ass.

Mona made her way to the sofa and laid back, pussy lips spread wide open, three fingers inside of herself to the view of the couple before her that was getting it on. She watched her husband who had only had sex with her since she'd known him, getting buck-fucked by a strong, sexy, woman who was giving them their first threesome.

Ten minutes went by and Athena continued her rhythm, fucking him while he fucked her back. She then lifted herself and moved her leg so she could face the other way. She sat on Marcel's wide dick from behind, her back to him, her ass bouncing in his face, eyeing Mona.

He watched Athena's skills and groaned, and looked over at Mona again.

She nodded yes while still pleasing herself like she was watching a porno movie. Sensing he had a mix of excitement and apprehension, she said, "It's okay, baby. Get you some pussy. Come for me. Come inside of her. That would turn me the hell on."

Mona began rubbing her clit faster and Athena fucked harder, and he looked up at Athena's defined back and fucked her deeper, grabbing on to her trim waist.

"Fuck!" Marcel screamed as he let out a deep grunt like he

was finally able, without guilt, to release the buildup of fluid that the other-woman-orgasm had brought on. It was as if traveling from his balls to his tip was more than he could take.

Athena let out a wail and said, "Oh hell yeah! Come with me!"

He did. He came.

She did. She came.

And voyeuristic Mona said, "Oooohh, shit. I'm coming, too."

By two in the morning, after two more rounds, Mona and Marcel were fast asleep, facing away from each other, knocked out.

Athena was gone.

They awoke earlier than normal and immediately began a headboard banging, morning breath kissing, I'll pee later, missionary fuck like no fuck they'd ever had before.

His words after they both ended up on their backs along the ebony Egyptian sheets, coming down from their morning sex intensity was, "See if she can come by again."

Chapter Five

A week had gone by and their ménage-a-trois had already happened pretty much every other night.

It was a Saturday afternoon. Mona and Marcel had gone to the gym and Mona was finished with her work out first. She sat at the smoothie bar waiting for Marcel, sipping on a strawberry banana protein shake, talking on her iPhone.

Athena sounded enthusiastic. "Your husband is amazing!"

"True." Mona had never heard anyone say that so intimately about Marcel, especially someone talking about her man's bedroom skills. She took a second to let the sentence settle, and then said, "You seem to handle it well."

"I try. Not to mention you and your talents," Athena said while driving in her car.

"Speak for yourself."

Athena asked, "Will you two be home tonight?"

"Yeah. You coming by?"

"I can."

"Good." Mona sipped her shake.

"It'll be a little later than usual. The guys are helping me move. We should be done by nine. They're coming at six."

"Move?"

"Yeah. Mona, truth is, I'm getting evicted. I got so far got behind in my rent that they wouldn't even take my money when I was able to give them part of it, so I just gave up. So, I've been saving, basically. But, the sheriff will be by any day now. I just wanna be honest with you."

"Girl, please. I understand . I got evicted once myself. It's no fun at all."

"No, it's not. I'll be staying at one of those weekly hotels."

"Okay. Sorry to hear that. Well, for tonight at least, when you come by, why don't you just spend the night?" Mona asked.

"Really?"

"Yeah."

"You sure? What about Marcel? You think he'd mind?"

"He'll understand. Plus, if you're not gonna be done until late, why pay for the full day at a hotel? It'll be fine."

"As long as you're sure."

"I am. You should've spent the night before now, but you always insist on leaving."

Athena said, "That's because I wanted to be home to make sure the Marshall's office didn't show up first and lock me out."

"I know that's right. You just bring yourself over when you're done. Park in the driveway, not on the street. We'll see you later." She stood when she saw Marcel approach.

"Thanks, boo."

"Bye."

*****

Athena's overnight bag was in the guestroom down the hall. The tan duvet was turned back for her arrival. But for now, she was in the master bedroom as usual. She was dressed in a skimpy, pale yellow teddy—pantiless.

The volume of the foursome porn movie stood in for soft music. On the screen were two couples swapping.

In the bed this time it was Marcel between Athena's legs, eating her out like a champ. He'd been devouring her for the past fifteen minutes. Mona was behind him at the edge of the bed, her mouth to his testicles. He moaned as if pleased from the sensation of being a receiver, and the taste of being a giver.

Athena was quiet, watching Mona's reflection in the dresser mirror. She didn't make a sound. She then looked over at the movie, rubbing her own jiggly breasts. She brought her left nipple to her mouth with ease and sucked it.

Marcel looked in awe, yet continued. He slid his tongue in and out as if it was his penis; using his hands to grab handfuls of her cheeks while licking her Y-trail. He waited for her to arch her back like Mona usually did when he'd eat her out. He licked the skin of her perineum upward and downward, and gazed up at her.

She looked unfazed.

He said to them both, "Come on over here," as he rose up while Mona backed away. He walked to the sofa and Mona was right behind him, butt-ass naked.

Athena got up and removed her teddy.

Marcel directed Athena to lie on her back along the sofa, with her pussy near the arm's edge.

Mona leaned over the arm with her face to Athena's vagina. Marcel stood behind Mona and grabbed his erection. Mona knew his next move and she stuck out her hips in the right position so he could enter her raw. She looked back at his entry.

"Yeah, that's my man's dick. Love that shit." She then

faced Athena, as Athena used her own hands to expose her clit, as if she even needed to. Mona went to town, pulling on it, making a moaning sound that vibrated against Athena's skin. She sucked with a tongue wiggle, and Athena wailed. "Oh damn. That's it."

Mona bounced her ass back against Marcel's crotch while he dove his dick in and out of her, watching the girl-on-girl action before him.

A minute later, Athena glanced over at the television screen, seeing a white man's long penis going inside of a woman's tight dark pussy, and Athena burst. "Uuuhhgh, ohhh, yes! Ohh, yes. Yes."

Marcel kept up his pace, feeling himself about to blow but he purposely slowed down. He took a step back and pulled out of his wife.

Athena said to Mona, "You can eat some pussy boo."

"Yes, she can," Marcel said, looking only half-proud of her. He then said, "Baby, sit on her face while I show her what we do."

Mona's eyebrows raised. "Oh, you mean what we do when I'm on my back, on the edge of the sofa?"

"Yeah."

Athena got up and laid on her back, bringing her hips right along the edge while Mona straddled her face.

Athena sniffed. "Oh, this pussy smells good."

"That's from all that dick stirring things up," Mona replied.

Marcel put on his condom and got on his knees on the floor, his hips to the height of Athena's hips. He grabbed on to her legs, hooked his arms under her thighs, and scooted her ass off the edge even further. He penetrated her and aimed his insertion upward and began fucking fast and steady, over and over, purposely guiding his tip to her soft spot.

Athena let out a groan that seemed to momentarily deter her from giving Mona an oral lashing.

Mona ran her fingers through Athena's short hair, and looked back every now and then to watch her man fuck. "Damn, this is sexy."

Before long, Athena was so distracted that she stopped eating all together, giving off more sounds like she was about to straight lose it. The more Marcel hit her pussy at the upward angle, the more she stuttered incomprehensible words. Then she managed to say loudly, "Oh no. Wait!"

He didn't.

He felt her walls repeatedly squeezing his dick and he yanked himself out. She grunted. There was the sound of a gush. Clear fluid spewed from Athena's vagina like it was sperm. It landed on his stomach and chest. He popped her clit with his hard dick and she squirted again.

"Oh fuck," she screamed, watching it happen. "What is that? I'm peeing on myself."

Mona looked back, watching too. "No you didn't. Girl, you squirted. That's just how we do it."

Marcel entered her again. He hit upward in the same way and she made the same Ungh, ungh, ungh, sounds again. He pulled out, popping her clit. She bore down and released again.

Then it seemed he could no longer contain his excitement. Marcel ripped off his condom, jerking himself off.

Mona got on her knees just in time and he came in her mouth.

"Damn," he said, heart beating fast to the thrill of having watched Athena enjoy her first ejaculation.

Athena looked lost and astonished. "Did that just

happen?"

Mona stood up, wiping her mouth. "It did."

Athena shook her head. "Hell, I'm not going anywhere."

"You shouldn't," Marcel said.

Mona said, "Damn. I've got the best of both worlds."

"So do I," he said, looking drained.

Mona kissed Marcel on his cheek. "That's my baby. Got that magic stick. Love my baby."

"Love you." His words were slow and low.

That night, Athena knocked out right where she was, on the sofa in their room under a mink throw.

****

By six in the morning, Marcel, who had a breakfast sales meeting at seven, got up and carried Athena to the bed, but not the bed in the guestroom, he took her to his and Mona's bed, placing Athena under the covers right next to Mona. He laid her on her stomach, just like Mona, and slapped both of their asses. They each looked back at him, giving him the sleepy eye.

He hopped in the shower and got ready for work with a newly converted smile on his face.

When he walked out of the bedroom he said, "I want you both here when I get home."

They said in unison, "Okay, baby."

Athena scooted closer to Mona and arranged herself in a manner to hold Mona in her arms. They both fell back to sleep.

Later, before the ladies left for the day they took a shower together with Athena on her knees. She looked up in lust and asked Mona if she could be their girlfriend, the three of them only sexing up each other. Mona agreed as she let out an orgasmic cry.

Mona, like Marcel, was in triangle heaven.

Chapter Six

It was late afternoon; two weeks after Athena's first squirting discovery. There had been more since then. Having her first vaginal orgasm called for many demand performances.

Mona was half-way through her nine-hour work shift from one o'clock to closing.

Each and every day since their decision to invite another woman into their bedroom, Mona's mind had been full of visual summaries of every position, sound, and feel of the experience she'd begged her husband to join in on. It was different in a good and bad way. That had her mind spinning.

She now had a man who was discovering the freakier side of his sex life with her permission, and she had a woman who could turn both of them on together. Against the grain of a conventional world, the possibilities were exciting to her. Although there was something deep inside that whispered a cautious tune. But what spoke louder was the fact that their sex life was hotter than it had ever been, and that the future possibilities with them walking on the wild side could be even hotter.

She felt her cell phone vibrate along her hip and she stepped aside, into the backroom of the store, answering it as she closed the door behind her.

"Hi, honey."

"Hey. What's going on?" Marcel asked.

"Not much. Just about to take a dinner break. I brought some leftovers. I think I'll heat up that lasagna."

"Okay."

"You home already?" she asked.

"Yeah, and baby, I want to ask you something."

"What is it?" she asked, wondering.

He spoke slow. "I know you told me you wanted me to get mine, that it's okay with you as long as we're up front. That if I'm happy, you're happy."

"Yes."

He took a moment. "Athena is here."

Mona took a second and swallowed hard. "She is? Why?"

"She said she thought you were home. She didn't know you worked the late shift."

"She could've called me. I would've told her." She walked toward the back of the room.

"Well, it turns out she left her cell phone here after she left at five this morning."

"I see." Mona's mind raced.

She could hear him take a long inhale and exhale. He said, "And, baby. I just wanna know something. Is it okay with you if Athena and I have sex? She was about to leave after she got her phone, and then, well...we didn't kiss, but we hugged each other goodbye and things got heated. She was about to walk out the door and I admit, I'm the one who closed it. She's upstairs."

Her eyes flashed question marks. "In our bedroom? In our bed?"

"Yes. I just want to be honest with you."

She folded her arms. "Marcel. Really?"

"Yes."

In her mind she said, Shit. Dammit. Fuck. Out of her mouth she said, "Well, I appreciate you telling me. That's the only way this will work. I've seen the two of you doing everything to each other you could ever do. Just remember what we talked about. No anal sex and no kissing Marcel. I mean it."

"I know."

She swallowed and sighed and then sort of said what she wanted to say. "It's fine. Go ahead. Enjoy yourselves. But not too much enjoying without me." She gave a weak chuckle.

His chuckle was strong. "Thank you."

Did he just thank me? "Okay. Call me when she leaves."

"I will."

"Bye."

"Bye." His bye had more energy than his hello.

She realized he hung up first. Mona didn't move. She thought about being a fly on the wall to the vision of his every footstep, up the stairs, into the room, and wondered which position they'd take on first. Would it be him sucking her toes or her giving him head or him fucking her missionary or him eating her out? But one thing she knew for sure. Mona knew Athena was going to get Marcel to make her squirt. The last time, he even alternated between them both, making them squirt one after the other. He had gotten good at knowing how to hook Athena up. But Mona's thoughts were on Athena getting hooked—period. Repeated great sex had a bonding factor and Mona knew it. She hoped Marcel would call within thirty minutes and it would all be over. She asked for it.

Mona went back on the floor and never ever clocked out for lunch. She decided she'd rather work than eat. Staying busy for thirty minutes, or two hours, depending on the next phone call from him, was the best medicine to keep her distracted. Distracted from the realization that her husband was having sex with another woman, in their bedroom, in their bed, and with her permission.

Damn.

She took her cell and sent a text to her friend Piper. Hi sis. Just want to know...Is Athena cool people. I saw her after your guy's party and we've been kicking it.

A minute later.

Worked with her before. We don't talk a lot but yeah, she's cool.

Thanks. Take care.

It was time for bed, just around 11:20 p.m., and Marcel was in the bathroom brushing his teeth.

Mona was at least okay with the fact that she got a call forty-five minutes after Marcel called to ask permission to hit his side-pussy.

She lay in bed wearing his boxer shorts and his blue and white, extra large Dallas Cowboys tee-shirt. She turned onto her stomach. She could smell the scent of pineapple on her pillow. She fluffed it up, reminding herself to change the sheets the next day, turning onto her side as Marcel climbed into bed. He turned off the lamp, only leaving the glow of the nightlight from the bathroom. He wore the same thing she wore, but she could have sworn he smelled like pineapple too as he got under the covers with her.

She looked at his face and was silent for a moment as he

laid on his back. She adjusted her leg over to his and played footsies, leaning in to place a kiss on his cheek. Since she was a little turned-on at the thought of his one-on-one with Athena, she placed her hand on his penis, rubbing it and sneaking her hand inside his boxers.

He yawned, looking tired and his penis agreed with him, not her.

Suddenly, Mona's phone rang from her purse that was on the dresser. Marcel pulled the covers off and Mona moved her leg as he jumped up to get it, but it stopped ringing.

"Who was it?" she asked.

He looked at her cell. "Athena." He put her iPhone back in her purse and walked back to the bed.

Then, his phone rang. He answered it fast after taking it from the nightstand. "Hello. Okay." He put the call on speaker.

It was Athena, who sounded cheery. "Hi Marcel. Hi Mona. This is your phone sex thank you."

"Thank you for what?" asked Mona.

"For being so cool. Both of you. Especially you Mona, for trusting me with Marcel today."

She replied, "Okay," looking unsure.

"I just have to ask. Marcel, did you eat my girl's pussy yet tonight?"

Mona was the one who said, "No."

Athena said, "Oh, we can't have that. I think it's time for the two of you to get in a sixty-nine. Marcel, you suck her pussy while she sucks your dick, and I'll talk you through it. Get up on her and stick that big dick in her mouth, upside down, until she chokes."

Marcel looked at Mona and Mona looked at Marcel. He said, "Okay." He set the phone down on the pillow and pulled down his boxers, then he turned toward the foot of the bed.

Mona turned flat on her back and took off her shorts. He climbed on top of her, his now stiff penis toward her chin.

Athena spoke like a 1-900 phone sex operator.

"You guys don't have to talk. Mona, all I want to hear is you moaning from swallowing that cock all the way down, taking your hand to the base to guide him in and out, squeezing the tip with a grip like he's plunging into my tight pussy. Marcel, you use your chin, nose, fingers, lips and tongue, and anything else you can to work that entire pretty pussy. When she sucks you, you suck her clit just right, because I want the two of you to come together. For me."

He said nothing; mouth full of pussy.

She said nothing; mouth full of dick.

"Mona, when I come back there I want to lay on my back while we face each other, me riding his dick and you sitting on his face while we shove our tongues down each other's throats, rubbing titties just before he gets off, and then we switch places and he comes inside of you, while I cum on his fine ass face."

Moments later, Marcel started sucking harder. Mona moaned soft at first and then louder.

Athena moaned like she was getting off by her own hands, and even before Marcel geared up, Mona released her orgasms with a shrill. She gave off a slow, weepy sound.

"Good girl." Athena's sounded pleased at what she heard.

Marcel backed his face away and spilled his load into Mona's mouth, assisted by the cheerleading of his other woman. "Yeah. There it is."

Mona took it all.

Athena said, "Very good. And when I get there tomorrow, I'm cooking dinner. Sleep tight."

She hung up.

Mona and Marcel still panted, still in position.

He said, "Damn. That was some kinky shit right there."

He climbed off of her, moved the phone back to its perch on the nightstand and got under the covers again, along with Mona, facing her.

Mona asked, "Baby, I wanna know. Did you make her squirt today?"

"I did."

She gave him a smile on the outside, almost as though it was okay on the inside.

A new lifestyle was born.

Chapter Seven

It was after work at 6:19 p.m. the next day when Mona sent Marcel a text message.

Get home fast. We're waiting.

This time, she was the one alone with Athena, having arrived home to find Athena waiting outside in her car with bags full of groceries, ten minutes ahead of their agreed time.

The kitchen smelled like garlic and shrimp. A Tamia CD played in the background. "If I Were You."

Mona had taken a long shower and changed into a red silk robe and fluffy house slippers. Athena wore a short pink dress and was barefoot.

Mona walked into the kitchen. "It sure smells good in here."

"Thanks, boo." Athena gave Mona a cheek-kiss as she passed.

Mona leaned against the counter. "Marcel should be here any minute."

"Good."

"He said he wants to go out. You wanna go with us?"

"Where?"

"Just to Plush downtown. Watch some go-go dancers. Maybe dance a little bit ourselves. We don't get out enough."

Athena nodded as she stood over the stove. "Okay. I can go. I'd need to get some clothes though."

"Oh. Well, maybe we can just go out for a drink nearby so you don't have to change. You look fine all the time no matter what you wear."

Athena stirred the pot of boiling pasta shells, looking back, "Thanks. Either way, works for me."

Mona stepped up behind Athena and hugged her around the waist. Athena put the lid on the pot and turned toward Mona, hugging her back. She eased Mona backward toward the counter and undid the tie of Mona's short robe. Mona was naked beneath it. Athena eyed Mona's golden body and then kissed her neck, easing her hand down to Mona's vagina.

Mona gave a soft sigh, giving a sultry look, rubbing Athena's short hair along the side of her head.

Athena inserted one finger while sucking Mona's nipple.

Then the door from the kitchen to the garage opened fast. Marcel spoke faster. "Damn. You all are mean. You can't send me a text like that. I almost had an accident."

Mona smiled. Athena's back was to him but she still did her duty.

He closed the door and put down his cell and briefcase, undid his tie, and stepped up behind Athena. He lifted up her dress, exposing her peach colored G-string and rubbed her ass.

A couple of minutes later, Athena was on her knees pleasing Mona on the left, and alternating to please Marcel on the right.

Marcel said, with his hands on his hips. "Now this right here is what a nigga needs to come home to."

The song was, "Stranger In My House."

****

A little after ten o'clock, the threesome sat at the bar area of the trendy nightclub called Plush. Mona let Athena wear one if her dresses. A silver mini-dress, and her lavender platform pumps.

Mona had on a tight, charcoal jumpsuit, and Marcel wore black pants and a white button up shirt.

The large, stylish club with three levels was crowded. They were on the second floor, sitting upon hot pink leather bars stools beneath crystal chandeliers, sipping red berry Ciroc and cranberry. The club's ambiance was fresh and trendy, and the hip-hop music was loud.

When the D.J. played "Champagne Life" by Neyo, Athena, who sat to the right of Mona, was the first one to leap from her barstool, singing and snapping her fingers. She took Mona by the hand and the two of them ran off to the dance floor laughing.

Marcel sat back and watched them, partly feeling like a king, like the man who could make every other man jealous.

The manager, a young urban looking man wearing jeans and a multi-colored Coogi sweater, walked over to Marcel.

Mona looked over and saw the man point at her. Marcel and the man talked.

Athena never saw him.

After a few songs, the ladies returned to Marcel and the three of them watched the go-go dancers, drinking until just after two in the morning.

When they got home, Marcel fell asleep, along with the sound of his ladies moaning. The mattress told on their motions, along with a buzzing vibration. Some kind of toy. Athena's drunken shrill hit a soft note like she fought to keep it down.

Marcel snuck a peek at his new way of life, and turned over while they finished. Minutes later, all of them were fast asleep.

Chapter Eight

By the next week, Athena had been by to see Mona and Marcel a couple of times, with the exception of some evenings that she needed to work late, or she'd go to her hotel room and search online for places to live, a couple of times she'd even go out.

One Thursday night, she came by with her overnight bag, prepared to stay. Mona told her she'd leave the door unlocked and for Athena to come on upstairs.

Marcel lay on his side. Mona lay on her back with her legs over his hips. Her ass was right next to his torso for direct penetration. She arched her back slightly and clenched her legs together, crossing her ankles behind his back. His hand was on her vagina, stimulating her clitoris with short strokes while his dick was inside of her. Sounds of her ass cheeks slapping up against skin filled the air.

"Ahhh, look at you two. Nice." Athena walked in looking excited. While fully clothed, she scooted close to Mona and put her head on Mona's bare belly, watching Marcel's hand movements. Her hand replaced his, then she used her mouth, still laying across Mona's belly, but with her head at the top of Mona's mound, licking while Marcel watched up close.

Soon, it was clear that the position they were in did the trick. Mona had a long, rolling orgasm. Her voice was a whiny whisper.

Athena stood up, walked over and pressed play on the Prince CD. The first song was, "If I Was Your Girlfriend." She slowly unbuttoned her blouse to the sultry music.

Marcel lay next to Mona, and they watched. Athena brought the wooden chair that was against the wall to the center of the bedroom. They were treated to a chair dance by Athena. She circled the chair and placed her foot on the seat while she rubbed all over herself.

If I was your girlfriend, would you remember, to tell me all of the things you forgot when I was your man?

Prince's sexy voice led her sexy body. Athena's eyes were on Marcel.

Five minutes later, Marcel sat on the chair. What had started out as a chair dance ended with him sitting with his legs apart. The only difference was that now Athena was on her knees between his legs sucking him down from his tip to his testicles; wrapping her lips and her hands around his width and length. She continued the drill while Mona lay in the bed, rotating her fingers along herself. Athena continued until she could tell that Marcel was ready to come. Just as Mona was prepared to get up and receive him, he simply grunted and let it out into Athena's mouth.

Athena didn't back away. "Ummm, ummm."

Mona knew by the look on Marcel's face that he had an orgasm, even though he didn't look at her. He only looked at Athena. When Athena finished swallowing his semen, she rested her head on his leg and he rubbed her hair. He closed his eyes. Mona ceased her masturbation and turned over to lay in her usual position in the middle of the bed. She asked, looking away from the intimacy of the two of them, "Athena, are you still staying?"

"Yes. Here I come." She got up and cuddled up behind Mona on one end.

Marcel scooted next to Mona, facing her.

Prince CD's played most of the night and no one, not even Mona who never slept, got up to turn it off. The night ended with the song, "Scandalous."

****

That morning, Mona got dressed while and Marcel and Athena were still in the bed. She nudged Athena on her shoulder. "I'm leaving now. You need to get up."

"Oh, I'm not going in until noon," Athena said sleepily.

"Marcel is going in late too."

"I know." Athena looked up and gave Mona a morning smile.

Mona didn't bother to return one. She insisted. "Athena, I'm about to leave. Leave with me."

"Oh, okay, boo." Athena read the look on Mona's face and got up.

About ten minutes later, Athena left and Mona still frowned. It was time to talk.

Marcel sat up in bed, all ears, bare-chested.

She said, "Honey, I noticed something. It seems the last few times she stayed over, she went in late, and you went in late." She stood over him.

"I think that's a coincidence, baby."

"I don't."

"What's wrong?"

"I'm gonna call her. I think we all need to talk." Mona had her cell in hand and dialed Athena, but she didn't answer. She said on her voicemail, "Please call me." She then sent a text, typing. Call me right away. "Damn," she said. She looked at Marcel with a frown. "Listen."

Marcel's phone beeped from the nightstand. He looked at the screen and said in response to what he saw, "Okay."

"What?"

"It's Athena."

"Why is she calling you and not me?"

"It's a text. A picture."

"Of what?"

"Her!"

"Let me see." Mona took his cell. "She sent you this? A picture of her bald pussy. Why?"

He shrugged his shoulders. "I don't know."

"I'm calling her again." Mona's phone beeped. She looked. "What the hell? She sent it to me too. We don't need that shit." Mona looked ready to go off.

"What is wrong with you?"

"What's wrong? You really have to ask? See, I really wanted to know how you would handle yourself in a situation like we're in. And honestly, I'm not sure this is working out."

"Why?" He looked puzzled.

"First of all, I can sense something. Just like last night, her swallowing you and resting her head on your leg. It's like the two of you forgot I was even in the room. Shit, I feel like she gets more dick than I do."

"No. The only time I really do her is when she wants to

squirt. Most other times it's oral on her part and you know she does that a lot to both of us."

"Whatever. I think she's bonding. Not to us, but to you. "

"I don't."

"I do! I know women." She began using her hands as she spoke. "Plus, it's obvious she's trying to stay with you while I'm gone. I'm not having it anymore. I was about to talk to you about her staying with us until she finds a place because I'm almost anticipating her next move to be to ask to live with us anyway. But there's no way in hell that's gonna happen."

"She said she found a place anyway. She moves in next week."

She tiled her head. "See, she told you that. Not me. You two are closer then she and I are. How'd that happen, Marcel?"

"Mona, I don't give a damn about her."

"I think you do."

"Well, I don't." He put his cell on the bed and readjusted himself.

"I'm willing to bet she sure thinks you do. And anyway, it seems like you've been getting home late on the very nights she can't come over. What's up with that?"

"I'm always home no later than eight. Her going out has nothing to do with me."

"It's odd."

He said, "It's accidental."

"Well, new rule. She can only be here when I'm here. Period."

"Okay. But why are you mad at me?"

She got loud. "Because, this is getting out of hand. You're getting a little too cozy with this whole idea. The first time I let you fuck her while I was at work, you weren't even in the mood to be with me until she called giving us phone sex."

"I would've been ready."

"You were yawning."

He spilled his words. "Mona. Come on now. You know this is on you. After all, this was your idea. You wanted to see me fuck another woman." He pointed at her. "You wanted her to be our girlfriend. You opened the door and asked me to do it. No, you begged me."

Astonished and pissed off best described Mona's expression. "Oh, hell no. Here we go. I never said that. I can't believe you're acting like this is my fault."

"You initiated it."

She leaned over him. "Did I initiate you coming in her mouth and blocking out the sight of me?"

He looked ready to get to it. "Please. I'm the one who was given all the rules and I've followed them. I watch you two come in each other's mouths, kiss and hug and dance together and hang out. Have I gotten jealous?"

Her hands found her hips. "Jealous? I'm the one being the coolest about the whole thing. I said go ahead and get your needs met, allowing you the freedom of not having to deal with a jealous wife so we can have a little fun. I guess that's not good enough for you. You don't want to be responsible enough to be sensitive to my feelings. You just want to point the finger at me like I asked for this."

"I do not."

She blinked fast. "You do. Besides, I could've been cool with it being one time. You're the one who said, 'hook it up again' and now I'd say she's getting addicted. This was about lust. Not love. To me it looks like you two are falling. Like your mind is blown."

"Yeah, right. She pleased me and you. I felt if this whole thing pleased you, it would be worth a try. I got over my nervousness, past my fear of you being mad at me for enjoying someone other than you, and you're still mad. I got invited in and ended up saying yes, but I was still worried that you'd be upset if I enjoyed myself too much. Your thing is, you enjoy watching me with her and then when that happens, you say I'm falling for the girl." He cut his eyes.

Mona stood up straight. "You enjoyed watching just like I did. But you two are together more than just the times when I watch. I know what good dick can do. It can make a woman go fucking crazy."

"Crazy is what I see right now. I think you're reading into this. Like just now, she sent us both the picture but you were ready to go off. You know what, let's just cut this whole thing off and never see her again. It's not worth it! You're right. It's not working." He came to a stance.

Her cell rang. She answered fast. "Hello."

Athena said, "Hey, boo. You wanted to talk to me?"

Mona's tone was dry. "I'm still at home. Trying to get out of here. I'll call you later."

There was the sound of traffic in the background. "Okay. I sent you both a little something. Plus I know the game is Monday night. I have some things to do this weekend, but on Monday I wanted to come by and make some chicken tacos. The three of us can just chill."

"We'll see." She watched a naked Marcel grab his underwear from the drawer. "But please, no more pictures. I'll talk to you later."

"Oh, okay. No problem. Talk to you then. Have a nice day."

Mona hung up and said, loudly, "Opening the flood gates means you get a flood. And yes, I opened them."

"Did we really get a flood?" he asked, heading to the

bathroom.

"You tell me."

He said with volume, "I can do without this. I was trying to put my focus on you, but to you, the focus has been on her. If you want her, she can be with you."

Mona said a firm, "Goodbye" and left.

Chapter Nine

All together; all relaxed.

It was a Monday night. The Cowboys played the Rams in overtime.

The Cooper's house smelled like home made tacos. Cans of Pepsi sat along the coffee table.

Marcel lay upon the left side of the sectional in the den with his back against the arm rest; his legs along the cushions.

Mona lay on her back, her head along his stomach with her legs stretched out. Her skirt was raised up to her waist.

Lying along Mona's stomach, with her mouth smack dab in between Mona's legs was Athena, licking Mona's cunt like she was lapping up a bowl of half-melted chocolate ice cream. Her finger held Mona's thong to the side.

Mona was in la-la land.

Marcel looked down at the two of them and returned his eyes to the game.

He massaged his woman's hairline and wiped her

forehead as Athena backed away and sat up. She said, "We can finish this later. There's more where that came from."

Mona leaned up with a smile and eased her body to the curve of Athena's shapely frame. They hugged as Mona placed a kiss on Athena's neck. Mona made sure to rest her leg across Marcel's to include him in the triangle of family love.

Their lifestyle continued.

Marcel only looked at the game. "Damn. How you gonna let him get through that hole?" An hour and a-half later, the Cowboys celebrated an overtime win.

Three hours later, 2:31 in the morning, the three settled into their post-sexual escapades position, with Mona in the middle, Marcel on her right, spooned behind her, and Athena on her left, facing her, their knees touching just so.

A phone rang. It was Mona's. She reached over Marcel's knocked out body to grab it, saying groggily, "Hello."

"Mona. This is Piper." Piper's voice was rushed and high. "You know that chick who came to the football party that you asked whether she was cool people or not?"

"Yeah."

"That bitch has been fucking Tyrone! And girl, I don't know if Marcel is near you or not, actually I really don't give a shit, but the pictures I just saw on Tyrone's iPad are of a threesome. Tyrone, that bitch Athena, and Marcel. Sucking and fucking."

Mona fought to wake up her brain that had to have been still asleep. She hoped it was. "What in the hell did you just say?" She reached over to turn on the lamp.

"I'll send these sick ass suckers to you. There's even a shot of them double-dipping. Tyrone fucking her pussy and Marcel in her funky ass."

"Oh, hell no!" Mona threw the phone who knows where,

only hearing the thud of it hitting up against something. She propelled her body from the bed.

"Bitch, get your ho-ass up, now!" She jetted to the side where Athena lay.

Athena's eyes were half open looking at Mona like she must be dreaming herself.

Mona shouted, "Wake the fuck up and get the hell out of my bed and out of my house before I blow your motha-fuckin head off!"

Marcel sat up fast, looking lost. "What in the hell is going on? What happened?"

"You, motha-fucka. You and her. Piper has pictures to prove that you two have been fucking behind my back and having a fuckfest with Tyrone."

"Baby, wait. She's wrong. It's not like that."

She aimed her fast moving, lethal words at Athena, who sat up with the sheet to her chin like she had a sudden burst of modesty.

"You get your ass out of here right now!" She pointed toward the door. Mona's face was beet red. One hand was balled up. "All you need is your car keys. Leave before I blow your freaking ass away. Talking about, 'it'll just be the three of us.' Your dirty ass can't even count!" Mona darted to the closet and reached up to the shelf, looking for the shoebox that held her .9mm glock.

Athena screamed as Mona rummaged through it. Mona grabbed the black handle of the handgun, put the magazine in and cocked it to load the round. Athena's screams grew fainter. She was down the stairs by the time Mona hurried back out of the closet. Mona aimed the steel barrel at her departure. Athena had taken off like a fire through a Jheri curl, snatching the sheet and her purse, and running out the front door naked, leaving it wide open.

Mona ran down after her to the sound of Athena's car starting up, then backing up and screeching away. Mona still aimed. She wanted to shoot Athena so bad her nipples got hard.

"You need to stop fucking and go get your daughter Bitch!"

Suddenly Mona heard his voice behind her. She turned toward Marcel and aimed the cocked and ready barrel at his bare chest.

He put his hands up. "Mona. No! Calm down. I can explain."

"Shut. The. Fuck. Up. Explain what? How your dick ended up in her ass? I sure hope you wore a condom, Marcel. My God. You had so much damn rope that you hung yourself. And your dumb asses did that shit and even took photos?"

"No. It wasn't like that."

"You...just get out! I don't care where the hell you go, but you need to leave. Even for thirty minutes, you need to go. Now! Don't test me." She spoke so loud she shook.

He took a step closer.

"Go Marcel."

He shook his head empathically. "No. You're gonna have to shoot me or call the police. I'm not leaving my house, and I'm not leaving you." He dropped his hands.

Her index finger was anxious, like it begged her to just give him one bullet to his enemy dick. "Move!" she shouted. "It's time to flip the script on your ass and get me two dicks at the same time."

He stepped away from the stairs, looking both stunned and anxious.

She ran up to their room and locked the door. That was when the tears began to fall. Her sudden yearning had led to unleashing the greedy, sneaky, pussy-hound in her husband. She yelled out loud, "Just like my horny ass father who snuck around on my mother every damn chance he got, saying she was too jealous, too smothering, and still, I end up with a man who can't handle the openness of his freedom." She roared even louder toward the door. "Your dumb ass still had to sneak and have the forbidden fruit. I never believed you were really being faithful before all this. Hell, what man can be?"

He yelled back from the other side of the door, "Me. I was. I was one-hundred percent faithful before this. Baby, I went by Tyrone's house after the owner of the nightclub said Athena was his boy Tyrone's girl. I wanted to know if it was true, I wanted to see if he was cheating on Piper and find out what the real deal was. Tyrone and I talked about what a freak she was. The next thing I knew, she showed up at his place and we both had her. I went back a couple more times when he texted me. I had no idea there was a camera setup. We opened a can of worms and got caught up. I'm sorry. Please forgive me."

Mona yanked the bedroom door open, holding her cell and an overnight bag in one hand, and the glock in the other; it was aimed at him. "One thing my mother was right about, she said don't let a woman in your house around your man; pretty soon she'll be in your bed and more. She said it's asking for trouble. I'm gonna have to go and tell her she was right!"

She pushed past him and ran downstairs, grabbed her purse from the kitchen counter, and left through the kitchen door; dialing her mom as she pulled out of the garage.

For Mona and Marcel, pleasure and happiness proved to be two different things.

Threesome curiosity had killed the cat.

The triangle backfired.

They were no more.

But not for long.

Later, after six months of Marcel pleading and wooing her back, Mona forgave him and they got back together.

Ten years of, if it ain't broken don't fix it.

There would be no more fucking fixing it.

Two turned out to be greater than three anyway.

Lethally Yours
By Niyah Moore

I rolled out of a luxurious queen-sized bed, naked, feeling as if I never went to sleep. My mouth was dehydrated; much like a desolate tract. The cavity of my stomach griped, pained, and cramped as I clutched it. My head pulsated as an unbearable hangover throbbed behind my temples. I hated this feeling. It was the feeling of a hangover. The vast quantity of alcohol I consumed the night before was to blame; but without the liquor, I wouldn't have been able to get through the night.

Taking a glimpse around the familiar lavish hotel suite, I noticed my clothes were sprawled out recklessly. I scratched the top of my itchy head. The expensive long jet black hair extensions were a mess. Fuck it, I thought. I had a hair appointment later anyway. I drug my dainty feet, feeling like a ton of bricks every step of the way, over to the massive window while trying to finger-comb through the tangles.

When I pulled back the curtains, I heaved a sigh of relief to find I was still in San Francisco. I hated waking up in another city. Nothing was worse than trying to figure out how to get back home when my mind couldn't put scattered pieces together. That was one of the many down sides to getting drunk on duty.

On the desk was a nearly emptied fifth of vodka. I picked up the bottle and downed what was left of it. Suddenly, I sneezed. Grabbing the tissue from a box on the nightstand, I blew my nose.

The reek of stale sex perturbed the air from the sheets, so I opened the window to get some clean fresh air. That's when the toilet flushed from inside the bathroom. The noise startled me at first.

I had forgotten that quickly that I wasn't alone.

The bastard was still there.

I tossed on the white hotel robe from the floor to swathe my nude body while hurling the tissue into the trash.

The short, husky, dark-skinned man came out of the bathroom, fully clothed in urban casual wear, baggy jeans, and a crisp white oversized t-shirt. His silver chain looked heavy around his thick neck. Even the large diamond bracelet on his left wrist was icy. Tattoos covered both forearms.

I remembered the motherfucker, but couldn't recall if my back arched or if he sweated like a pig when he fucked me. I took a seat on the bed and lit a cigarette crossing my legs as I pondered. The soreness I felt was a sign that he showed no mercy when he gave me his sex.

He retrieved his wallet from his black leather jacket, took a crisp one hundred dollar bill out, and extended his hand. Cheap bastard, I thought. I avoided his hard overindulgent eyes and pointed to the nightstand instead. He placed the money on the nightstand and adjusted his coat. His eyes traveled up my legs, then stopped at the cleavage that was exposed through the open part of my robe. I untied the robe so he could get a better look.

He licked his lips and shook his head.

"Last night...you were something else," he said positing himself between my legs. "I haven't had sex that good in a long time. Is it cool to give you a call if I need to see you again?"

"Sure," I replied, taking a puff from the cigarette, and putting it out in an ashtray from the nightstand.

He placed his right hand in my robe, squeezed my breasts, and traveled between my thighs. I spread my legs for him and leaned back on the bed extending my hands to grasp the pillow above my head. Fondling and exploring me again, with his eyes closed, he made his way to easing his fingers inside of me.

When he opened his eyes, he froze. He wanted to say something, but couldn't because the fact that I had a nine millimeter with a silencer pointed straight to his head made it hard for him to talk. I scooted back to get his disgusting fingers out of me.

Before he could blink, I pulled the trigger. The bullet went through the center of his big dome. His flesh and membranes splattered everywhere as his body fell to the floor. The stench of him losing his bowels was going to fill the room in a few seconds, so I jumped up, put the gun in my purse, and proceeded to the bathroom. My head throbbed again causing me to pop three extra strength aspirin. I dressed as quickly as I could, grabbing my leather jacket before slipping into my three-inch stilettos before leaving the room.

He didn't see death coming. That's what made it so exquisite. He thought I was just some bargain-basement-priced prostitute.

Wrong!!!

He was a target.

I was the hit woman.

His own wife, a woman who was tired of the abuse she suffered from his hands, wanted him dead.

Shaking off the icy chills that tried to come over me, I kept it moving. I hated to sleep with the bastard before blasting his brain out, but that was the only way to get this one. Good pussy was a man's kryptonite.

Sam, my personal bodyguard, waited outside the door. I paid him fifteen hundred dollars to watch my back and get rid of any evidence. We grew up together in Lakeview. He couldn't find a job when he got out of the penitentiary, so I hooked him up. His big arms, tall frame, and hard unbreakable intent look would make anyone shit in their pants. He went into the room to clean up while I went down to the first floor to return the hotel key.

I checked out of the room that was listed under a false identity, and then made my way to the parking garage underneath the Parc 55 Wyndham Hotel in Union Square. The air was chilly, even inside the garage, so I put my leather coat on to keep myself from shivering. I lit a cigarette and when I was almost finished smoking it, Sam met me. I tipped him the hundred dollar bill the bastard gave to me before I threw on my shades.

I nodded at him. He nodded back. I got into the brand new Infiniti. He watched me until he couldn't see me anymore.

That was a typical morning after one night working. I, by no means, deliberated twice concerning people I executed. I was too deep into the game to feel shame.

****

"Damn, baby, you look good in that fur," My husband, Donovan, admired while I tried on and modeled a blue Chinchilla for him.

"You like this?" I asked turning around in a circle.

Donovan didn't mind giving me anything I wanted, whenever I wanted it. Since he was a Senior Project Manager of a very big construction company in the city, he could afford it.

His eyes admired the way I looked in the fur coat. He smiled with his perfect white teeth shining. That smile was part of the reason why I married him.

"Of course I like it. Turn around again for me." He rubbed his chocolate covered hands together and slowly drank me in from head to toe like I was his favorite beverage.

I giggled like a schoolgirl as I moved my hair over my shoulder, turning very slowly.

Donovan's eyes were glued to my curves. He shook his head saying, "It's a shame how much ass you have." With a quick swat of his hand, my ass shook behind me.

I turned to the sales clerk and uttered, "I'll take it."

It was amazing how he could still make me swoon and be the man of my dreams. Our love wasn't perfect. I mean, we bickered, argued, and sometimes went to bed without speaking to one another. But, for the most part, we were happy and in love.

Donovan walked to the front of the store whipping out his credit card. While I removed the coat, my cell phone rang. When I saw it was my partner calling, I walked to the front of the store, so Donovan wouldn't be able to hear me.

"This is Sage Hunter."

"Sage, where are you?" Tank asked.

"I'm lying low...with my husband. Why?"

I silently prayed she wasn't calling me for another job. I really wanted to quit for the sake of the family I wanted to create with my hubby; but I knew Tank wouldn't understand.

"Miami, tonight..." she said.

"I can't...I'm celebrating my fifth wedding anniversary with Donovan. Plus it's already four o'clock in the afternoon. I would have to get on the very next flight in order to make it there by this evening."

"You just make sure you're in Miami before midnight."

I sighed heavily into the phone feeling pressured. "After this, Tank, I'm done. I can't continue to live like--"

She hung up on me in mid-sentence. Donovan kissed me sweetly on my neck. I smiled and turned to face him putting the phone into my pocket.

"The coat is being boxed up to take home," he said. "I can't wait to see the gift you're getting me."

Worry instantly filled me as I stared into his eyes, but I didn't show it. How was I going to tell him that I had to leave him home alone on our celebration night? And where would I tell him I had to go?

"Happy Anniversary baby doll," he said unable to detect there was a problem. He gave me a quick peck. "What you want to do now?"

"Let's go to Miami."

"Miami?"

He didn't know what I did for a living, but he had all kinds of wild ideas. At one time he thought I was a stripper, but he couldn't prove that. Another moment in time, he thought I made up a job to mask an affair. A steady income was the only proof of a job I had.

"Let's get away. Shit, let's just be spontaneous."

As I placed a soft sensual kiss on his lips, his tense

shoulders dropped a little bit. I hated to bring him along, but I really wanted to spend quality time with him for our anniversary.

"Hmmm, we've never been there. I hear Miami is sexy. We can go salsa dancing and make love on the beach. That's a good idea."

After taking the box from the clerk, we walked out of the store to get into a cab. It didn't take long to find one. They were lined up outside waiting for customers. We walked to the front of the line and got into the first one on the curb.

"Take us to Steiner Street by Alamo Square Park," I said to the cab driver.

My mind was in a million places. I was worried about taking him along with me on a job. All of my jobs had worked out smoothly without any mess. It would be horrible if this one time things didn't go as planned. I bit on my fingernails, something I did when my nerves were trying to get the best of me.

Donovan asked, "Why do you really want to go to Miami tonight?"

There was no way I could lie to Donovan. Hiding my occupation was one thing, but he knew something was wrong. "I have to work," I confessed.

He dropped his head and made a "tsk" sound. Disappointment filled his eyes as he tried to focus on something out of the window. With his saddened mood affecting my nerves even more, I decided to look up the flight schedule from my cell phone. We had a little over an hour to get to the airport if I wanted to make the very last flight. Donovan continued to stare out of the window and I could see his thought process as he chewed on the inside of his jaw.

Taking his hand in mine, I tried to get him to look at me,

but he refused. I wanted to quit my job, but it hadn't been easy for me. I started out avenging the homicide of my identical twin sister, Sadie, but it led to much more. Tank, a friend I confided in for backup, saved my life when the punk that murdered my sister almost drowned me. I owed her. Together, we started a business of assassinating men who abused women.

My jobs were never drawn out because I always got straight to the point. No fighting, no war, and no mess.

One shot and it was a wrap.

I had extensive gun training and was more than qualified to handle any situation.

"Today marks the fifth year of the same shit," he expressed as he rubbed the top of his head with his right hand.

"What are you talking about?" I asked, even though I knew exactly what he meant.

"I'm tired of you traveling all over the place."

I hated to keep so many secrets from him. He didn't know I made nearly ten thousand dollars a job because I put the bulk of my money in an unknown account in Mexico.

"Look at me..."

His dark eyes finally met mine. "Baby, why do you have to work on our anniversary weekend?"

"I need you to understand. I'm going to handle my biz and then we're going to enjoy our anniversary in beautiful Miami. Do we have a deal?"

"How can I understand something when I don't know what you do? I mean, like, what is your occupation? I never knew a job that required people to travel to all these random ass places sporadically. A day here, two days there, then for two months no work, but then you go back. What husband would feel comfortable not knowing what his wife does for a living?"

"I know, babe. It's crazy."

"I'm beginning to drive myself insane over this. Why can't you just tell me what you do?"

"I wish I could, but I just can't."

"You must work for the CIA or something," he responded searching my eyes to see if his new guess was right.

"Even if I did, Donovan, it would be classified information. Trust me. I don't want to live like this anymore. I'm going to quit after tonight."

He raised his eyebrows. "You really want to?"

"It's time for us to start a family; don't you think?"

We hadn't talked about having kids in a long time. I was pretty sure he was close to giving up on the idea. The way his eyebrows went up and down, I knew he was happy.

"Aw babe, I would love to start a family. I can take care of us financially."

I nodded. "True."

We pulled up in front of our Victorian two-bedroom home. He paid the cab while I unlocked the front door, made a mad dashed into the bedroom, and started packing my bags. Donovan came into the bedroom with the boxed coat in his hands, placed it on the bed, and started packing his own things.

*

As soon as the hubby and I were checked into the hotel room, Donovan fell back on the bed feeling jet-legged after the non-stop seven-hour flight. I straddled and kissed him sensually. We were going to make the best of this situation and enjoy our anniversary.

He laughed at how roughly I was pulling his shirt over his head. "Whoa, baby, what's the rush?"

"I have to get out of here in a little while, so I'm trying to get it in." I unbuckled the belt of his jeans.

He stopped my hands. "I can wait until you get off work so we don't have to rush. Tonight is a special night and I want to make love to you nice and slow."

I moved his hands above his head with force and held them down as I slipped my tongue into his mouth. Between kisses, I said, "You know that beautiful Chinchilla you just bought for me?"

"Yeah," he breathed hard with anticipation.

"This is my thank you...so lay back, relax, and enjoy me."

With one fluid motion, I managed to take my shirt off. He unfastened my bra and tossed it to the floor. I jumped out of my clothes and so did he. He was moving so fast, he tripped on his jeans and landed with his back on the floor.

"Ouch." He laughed.

I slinked down on top of him and smothered his laugh with a passion-filled kiss.

We managed to get off the floor and collapsed on the bed clumsily while still kissing. As I straddled him, I put him inside of me with haste. He moaned as I grinded on him before moving up and down.

His hands took hold of my ass and guided me to slow down. "You're going to make me cum if you don't slow down baby."

I listened to his warning and slowed down my rapid pace, but not by much. He was a thorough kind of lover. As much as I loved that part about him, sometimes I wanted him to fuck me hard and fast. I didn't care if he was going to explode within a few minutes. It didn't take me long to get mine anyway. All I needed was a few minutes.

I bounced harder, watched him bite on his lower lip while grasping the comforter in his hands. He was fighting to hold his orgasm in. He drew in short deep breaths to prolong it.

Both of my hands went to his muscular chest and I dug my nails softly into his skin. Licking my lips and closing my eyes, I could feel him thrusting up into me with flaming vivacity. A sensual long moan escaped from within him. This was his pussy and only his. Nobody could rock me like him, and I needed desperately for him to help me forget about the night before.

Suddenly, he flipped me on my back and growled low and sexy; imitating a Lion. With soft kisses between my thighs, I knew what he wanted to do next. Before I could protest because of our time restraint, he started making love to my pearl with his tongue. I grabbed hold of the top of his head and squirmed underneath him to fight the tickling feeling. He was beginning to drive me crazy by the way his tongue was flickering. I tried to scoot up towards the headboard, but he chased and sucked me until I erupted.

I gasped for air as a series of trembles took over my body.

Donovan came up and kissed me fervently as he re-entered my dripping wet center. "Mmmmm," he muttered.

I wrapped my arms around his back as he gave me profound long strokes. Staring up into his eyes, I could see his love for me as he peered down at me. I moved my hips underneath him creating a friction that became combustible. His nose touched mine and sweat beads began to form on our bodies. We breathed in the same air, became one, and held on to our orgasms, not wanting it to end just yet.

Tantric sex was a favorite of ours. The art of making love through touching, breathing, and prolonging the moment was something that kept our magic magnificent on many occasions.

He bit on my lower lip, tugged it towards him, and then sucked it before French kissing me. Just when I was enjoying his good kiss, he moved his fiery lips down my neck and didn't stop making his trail until he got to my right nipple.

While still moving in and out, his mouth became a suction cup. That tongue went to work and I thought I was losing my mind.

"Oh, sweet Jesus," I called out as my stomach started feeling like a small quake was happening.

To the next breast he went as he burrowed his dick deeper inside of me. As he went in, he cursed, "Shit..." He went out. He went in. "Shit!!!" I knew he was getting ready to bust.

I was right there with him moaning and whimpering all the while. Faster and harder he went to get me to holler out his name, "Donovan!"

At the same time, we climaxed, and shared an orgasm. He lay between my legs while still inside of me, with his ear on my chest, and listening to my rapid heartbeat. I kissed the top of his head before caressing it.

Glancing at the clock, I realized it was almost nine thirty. I didn't have much time to get to work. If I basked in the moment for too long, he was going to fall into a deep sleep while lying on top of me.

I scooted from underneath his sweaty skin. Before I could get out of the bed, he tried to pull me back.

"Uh unh, babe, not yet..." he groaned.

"Sweetie, as much as I would love to...you know I gotta go."

"Fine, but when your ass get back, it's on and popping."

"You got it." I crawled out of bed and went into the bathroom to take a fifteen minute shower.

I dressed in jeans and a t-shirt before tossing my club

wear into a small duffle bag. I was going to have to change after leaving Donovan.

"Alright, babe, I'm off to work..."

He was snoring loudly and looked so peaceful that I didn't want to wake him. I tiptoed out of the room. Smiling, I walked to the elevator. On the way down to the lobby floor, the aftershock of good sex hit me. My clit tingled with every step in my stride, I bit on my lower lip to try to stop it, but it was no use. Donovan's dick always felt as if it were still inside of me, even hours later.

*

Club Amnesia was the spot. I arrived right on time. Scanning the place, I realized the person I was there for hadn't showed up just yet. I blew air from my lips and looked around for a flunky, someone to hold a conversation with until the man of the hour turned up.

There was a small group of five chatty men in suits at the bar; all decent in the looks department. I walked over with a strut and all eyes were on me. To break up their sudden silence I asked, "Excuse me, can I sit here?"

At the bar, there were plenty of other seats because the club wasn't packed. Without rejecting me, they cleared the space and allowed me to sit smack dab in the middle of them.

"Can I buy you a drink?" asked the Caucasian man with light green eyes and brownish-blonde hair.

"Sure. I like Cosmos." I flirted with a smile.

While he talked to the bartender, I gave the club one more look over as my plan of execution played in my head. Taking note of all exits and how many people were there.

"What are you guys up to tonight?" I questioned.

"Just hanging out," the Latin one wearing a Fedora hat answered. "Are you from around here?"

"No, what about yall?"

"We're from The Bronx."

"New York?"

The all nodded as they drank their brews from tall glasses.

"Where are you from?" The man who bought me a drink asked.

Taking my drink from him I replied with a lie, "Philly."

"Cool. You come alone?"

"No, my home girls are around here somewhere," I said looking around as if I really had some friends with me.

"You should round them up to come chill with us."

I drank with my eyes watching the front door as I nodded and smiled.

The target walked in. I clutched my purse feeling the nine that was tucked away inside. He stood about five feet eight inches tall, with light brown skin and dark eyes; he was wearing jeans with a black blazer over a white dress shirt.

His name was Ahmad. He walked to the other side of the bar. I noticed right away that the man was too fine to kill. His minor infidelity, I felt, was too petty, but his fiancé's final request was to make sure he didn't make it to the altar in the morning because he cheated on her with one of her cousins. Tank usually never took these jobs because women who dealt with cheating men always took them back, but the money was doubled and the woman was serious.

"Let me get a rum and coke," he ordered as he sat.

He was waiting for his boys to join him to celebrate his last night being a bachelor; only they weren't going to make it. A text message told them Ahmad was going to be at The Flamingo Club on the other side of town.

While the bartender fixed his drink, I stared in Ahmad's direction. He couldn't help but notice the way I crossed my legs in my mini-skirt. My eyes traveled him from head to toe before quickly returning to the gentleman that was trying to entertain me with his corny ass jokes. I faked a laugh at whatever he said with my hand over the top of my cleavage.

I could feel Ahmad's eyes, so I batted my eyelashes at him softly, trying to give him the green light to approach me. My perfectly arched eyebrows were raised and my glacial brown eyes told him I was interested. I waited for him to break his long stare first, but he couldn't take his eyes off me.

Suddenly, he looked guarded when the man I was with turned to see who I had my eyes on. I winked at Ahmad and he relaxed with a smile while tilting his drink my way.

The Caucasian stranger ended our conversation politely and walked away. I finished the last of my drink going over my plan of action in my head. By the time I looked down the bar, my target disappeared. Where did he go? I tapped the bar lightly hoping I didn't get too distracted and lose him. I was hoping to hurry up to get this over with. I couldn't wait to get back to my husband.

Ahmad whispered in my ear while placing money on the bar, "Let me buy the next round."

"Thank you Mister…"

"Ahmad… My name is Ahmad. What's your name?"

"Sage."

"That's a pretty unique name."

"Thank you."

"What are you drinking?"

"I'm drinking a Cosmo." The urge to pee surfaced. I really didn't want him to leave my sight, but drinking always made me have to go, and my bladder was too weak to hold it. "Hey, I'll be right back. I have to go to the ladies room."

"You're not going to take off and leave, are you?"

"I promise I'll be right back, but only if you stay put yourself."

His eyes were stuck on my body as I walked away from him with a sashay to the bathroom. I knew he was more than interested in making me his last conquest before tying the knot. I turned to smile at Ahmad. He smiled back.

On the way to the bathroom my cell phone started ringing. Shit, I wasn't prepared to talk to my husband. I knew if I didn't answer, he would be pissed. So, I went into the quiet stall before answering, "Hey, baby, is everything alright?"

"Hey, honey. I was knocked out, wanted to kiss you before you left."

"I didn't want to disturb you. I know how much energy that flight took out of you. Plus, our session was intense. You okay?"

"I'm good. How long will you be working tonight?"

"About two or three hours and I'll be heading back to you."

Donovan spoke softly, "Mrs. Hunter, I can't wait to get you back in this bed, so try to see if you can leave early...I'm getting bored."

"Don't worry sweetie, I promise I'll be right there. Try to enjoy the beautiful view from the room or go grab some dinner from that restaurant on the corner."

"It's raining... but, I am starting to get hungry. I'll have to check it out."

"Yeah, it was starting to sprinkle when I left."

"The news said it's hurricane weather. Why in the hell would they have you out here during hurricane season Sage?"

I had to pee so badly, I kept the phone close to my ear as I hiked up my skirt, ease down my panties, and took care of my business.

"Why is the phone echoing like you're in a bathroom?" he asked.

"Babe, I have to pee."

He listened, seemed like he was waiting to hear my pee leave me and be released into the toilet before speaking. "Okay, well, I'll probably grab some dinner in a minute...where are you working? Somewhere close by?"

"You know I can't disclose that information. It's top secret."

"Oh yeah...top secret..." He sighed heavily.

At that moment, I could picture him biting the inside of his jaw, eyes clouding up with frustrated tears, and that right hand rubbing the top of his head.

I said sweetly into the phone, "I love you."

He didn't hesitate when he replied, "I love you too."

"I'll see you soon."

"Yup." He hung up.

I put the phone into my bra, wiped, and flushed the toilet. I adjusted my clothing before leaving the stall. As I washed my hands, I looked at myself in the mirror. Switching up my posture, I checked my makeup and hair. I still looked cool. I exited the bathroom and scanned the club. More people had filled up the place.

Through the dancing crowd I could see Ahmad looking in my direction to make sure I was going to return to his side. I smiled and he smiled back as I walked towards him. He quickly took a look at the time on his cell phone.

"Are you waiting for someone?" I asked.

"I'm waiting for my boys. Tonight I'm celebrating my last night as a single man."

"Is that right?" I eased up onto the barstool and brought my lips to the cocktail glass. "You're getting married?"

"First thing in the morning, so I better not get too wasted."

He stared at my ring finger. Shit, I forgot to take my ring off. "I see you're already married."

"Going through a bad divorce," I lied easily. "I wear the ring in hopes that he'll come back home, but unfortunately, he has yet to return."

He shook his head as if he could feel my made up pain. "I'm sorry to hear that. A woman as beautiful as you doesn't deserve that."

I smiled and sipped my drink. I really needed a few shots. "Excuse me, bartender, can I get a double shot of Patron?"

"Damn lil' mama," Ahmad said. "Are you trying to get fucked up tonight?"

"It takes more than this to get me fucked up," I replied. "You want a shot? Let's get you a shot to send you off right."

"I'm not done with this one yet."

"You can finish that one after the shots. Don't tell me you're a pussy."

He looked at me as if I were crazy. "Hell no...let me get one too," he signaled to the bartender.

As soon as the shots were on the bar, we picked them up, clinked glasses, and I exclaimed, "Bottoms up!"

Patron was always smooth going down and I didn't feel the burning sensation until it reached my stomach.

"Whew!" he yelled over the music making an ugly face at how hot the drink felt going down his throat.

I laughed at him. "Are you alright?"

"I'm good."

As soon as he turned his head to look at the door, I slipped a few drops of a sedative drug, a combination of Gamma-Hydroxybutyric Acid and Rohypnol, into his rum and coke. Before he could put his eyes back on me, the tiny bottle was already in my purse. It wasn't enough to knock him out, but enough to make his head spin.

"Maybe you should call your boys and tell them not to come, so you can take me back to your room."

"Maybe I should. They're late anyway." He picked up his drink and took a big swig. "I have no idea where they are."

I tilted my glass towards his and danced in my seat. "I'm feeling it now."

He smiled and shook his head slowly as a thought entered his brain. "I can tell you're not going to let me leave this club without you."

"Why you say that?"

"The way you're staring at me with those beautiful brown eyes, got me feeling like I don't want to get married tomorrow. You're fine as fuck. You know that, don't you?"

I smiled and licked my lips. "I don't think that way about myself at all."

"You're dangerous..."

"You can tell that, huh?"

"Yeah." He nodded slipping his arm around my waist. "Do you mind if I touch you?"

I faced him in the stool with my hands gently pulling his jacket towards me. As my legs parted open, he slid right between my thighs. "As a matter of fact, I want you to touch me."

With a sly grin, he said, "I like that."

He downed his drink nervously as my hand moved down to the growing bulge in his pants. Seduction was easy with him. I almost felt as if I didn't have to slip him the date rape drug. After he put the empty glass on the bar, he moved his hands to the outside of my mid thighs.

I pulled him closer so I could whisper in his ear. "You

want to get out of here?"

He nodded and stared into my eyes. Didn't take the drug long to enter his system. He seemed a little confused as he wiped the sweat that was starting to slide down the side of his handsome face.

"Damn, I'm going to have to pause. I must've drank that way too fast, went straight to my head."

"Have a seat," I said patting the stool next to me.

He squeezed me tighter shaking his head in protest. "I'm cool. Hey, your lips look juicy as fuck right now. Can I kiss them?" Before I could answer, his lips were on mine and his tongue was inside my mouth. It was the sloppiest kiss I ever had. I thought as he twirled his tongue in and out of my mouth. He moaned, "You want to come with me? I have a room a few blocks from here."

I wiped my mouth. "I thought you'd never ask."

After I eased my body off the stool, he took my hand in his. He walked tall with confidence, but by the time we reached the front door, he started to look shaky. I wasn't sure if he was going to fall or not, so I walked firmly in my heels to keep him up.

Ahmad stumbled out of the club laughing at his own drunken silliness. We walked past everyone waiting in line and entered into a dark alley on the side of the club. "My car is r-i-i-i-g-h-t this w-a-a-a-y," he slurred.

The ground was wet, but rain was no longer falling from the sky. I tried to avoid the puddles, but Ahmad's clunky shoes were splashing the water all over my bare legs and that shit was cold.

"Okay..." I replied letting go of his arm. "Let's try to avoid the puddles."

He didn't answer, he was too fucked up to pay attention

to where he was walking as he trotted ahead of me.

Taking a look around to see if there was anyone in the alley, I put my silencer on the nine millimeter inside of my purse. Walking slowly with a few feet between us, I made sure the gun was cocked and the safety off.

"Come on...let's get out of here. I'm ready to fuck the shit out of you," he shouted back at me.

I looked around again, stalled, and made up something quickly. "Hold on, my shoe just got caught on..." My heels clicked against the wet pavement imitating a panic. "Damn it...hey, help me!"

He turned around to see what was holding me up. The lady in distress act always worked. I aimed the gun at his heart.

"What the--"

I shot him in the heart, not giving him a chance to ask his question. He landed face first into a small pool of water. I went to him, kicked him with the heel of my stiletto to make sure he was dead. Ahmad tried to crawl away as he whimpered. I shot him in his back two more times. He didn't move or make another sound. I bent down to check his pulse from his wrist. He was dead.

Before I could tuck the gun away in my purse, I heard a rustling behind the garbage can a few feet behind me and realized I wasn't alone in the alley. Someone or something was there. I lifted the gun back up and made my way over to the side of the garbage can.

As my heels clicked on the cement, I cocked the gun. The shadow of someone behind the can moved. I aimed and let off a shot, hitting the brick wall directly above that person. I heard the shell hit the ground. I had good aim and could've shot him in the head if I wanted to, but I didn't want to kill whoever it was. I just wanted to scare them.

When the person didn't run or make a sound, I whipped my body around the can, gun leading me, and we came face to face.

"Donovan?" I asked while lowering my gun cautiously. "Baby, what are you doing down here? How'd you find me?" Without answering me, he stared at the dead body lying in the middle of the alley behind me. "You saw the whole thing?"

He nodded and said without delay, "I tracked you using the new GPS systems on our phones. I saw you sitting at the bar with this man, and when you went to the bathroom, that's when I called you."

I closed my eyes tight, felt my throat tighten up, and my heartbeat thumped. I opened my eyes to see his frightened expression. I had forgotten all about that crazy app we had just put on our new phones to keep track of one another in case of an emergency.

"You weren't supposed to find out like this." I quickly hid the gun back into my purse.

His eyes watched everything I was doing. "This is your job?"

I nodded slowly feeling a little guarded. I wasn't sure if he was going to start an argument and leave or what.

"Why'd you kill him?"

I answered honestly. "I'm contracted to kill men who cheat on their wives or abuse them in any way, shape, or form."

Swallowing the hard lump in his throat, he then asked, "Were you the one that killed your sister's boyfriend?"

"Yes...when he got off for killing her, I couldn't let him get away with it."

His eyes went back to Ahmad's lifeless body. With his mouth slightly parted, his mind was working overtime. "I thought you were cheating on me. I thought you were making up some job to be with someone else...the way you were all over him had me ready to kill him myself."

When I touched his shaking hands, he jumped a little.

"Are you afraid of me?"

With his eyes searching mine, he drilled, "How many men have you killed?"

"That was body number twenty-two."

"... How much do you get paid?"

"Some jobs vary. This job was twenty-thousand."

He looked floored as he asked, "Where's the money?"

"The money is in an account safe in Mexico."

Suddenly, he pulled my body close to his. "I'm not going to lie to you. My heart feels like it's going to jump out of my chest..."

"Are you afraid?" I asked again feeling his body shake against mine.

"I'm rattled. I don't know this person, but I'm just glad you're not cheating on me." He laughed a little, but then his wide eyes looked terrified at the same time.

Shaking off the awkward moment, I snapped back to reality. We were still standing near a dead body. I looked around to make sure we were the only two in the alley. Grabbing hold of his arm, I said, "Come on."

We walked quickly in the opposite direction we came, in the shadows of the darkness, and out of the alley.

"Babe, your marksmanship is smooth as fuck."

I spotted a cab and flagged him down. "Are you saying you don't want me to quit?"

The yellow cab stopped. We walked to it.

"That's up to you. Now that I know your secret, it's safe with me."

Donovan reached to pull the handle of the car. I grabbed

his hand roughly before he could open it. "I hope so...I wouldn't want to have to get rid of you too."

He swallowed hard and studied my seriousness. With his free hand, he moved my straight long hair over my shoulder.

"I wouldn't want that either." He kissed me hard as if he were turned on by his discovery. We parted and my grip on his hand relaxed. "Damn, baby, you would really kill me? You're lethal."

I stared into his eyes with a stern look. "I'm lethally yours."

"Indeed...you're lethally mine."

"Let's go."

He opened the cab door for me so I could slide in. Once he was inside, he gave the Jamaican cab driver our hotel's coordinates, and then stared back at me. He shook his head in disbelief slowly and smiled a little.

I searched his eyes to see if I could tell if he was really okay or just maybe going through shock. His grin became wider. His nerves seemed to have calmed down.

"I know this may sound crazy or strange, but baby, seeing you in action did something to me."

"What did it do to you?" I quizzed.

"I'll show you as soon as we get back to the hotel."

I leaned against him, rested my head on his shoulder, and stared out of the window. Felt like I could breathe again. We rode in silence for the rest of the way. He paid the cab driver and we headed up to the room.

As soon as we were out of the elevator and onto the floor of our room, he pulled me roughly against the wall. He put his hand between my thighs, parted my legs open in my mini-skirt, and slipped his fingers beneath my panties. While his eyes were on mine, he played with my clit with his middle finger.

I closed my eyes as my own tense body loosened up.

"Open your eyes," he commanded. "I want you to look at me."

I did what I was told. He bit on his lower lip before kissing me. Right there, in the hallway, he finger fucked me. Before I could explode, he lifted me up and carried me to the room.

He maneuvered the plastic room key out of his pocket, opened, and closed the door easily. With his lips back on mine, he leaned me up against the wall behind the door, taking my panties completely off. He lifted my legs to wrap around his waist as he unbuckled his pants. He took them off. I didn't take my eyes off him as he placed himself inside of me.

As soon as my tight wet center opened up for him, he thrust hard and deep. The power of his stroke was unfamiliar, physical and more intense than what I was used to. Suddenly, he spun me around and bent me over.

"Grab your ankles!"

Excitement filled me as I obeyed. He entered, stirred a little, and then pumped hard creating a smacking sound against my ass. I moaned loudly. My nipples got hard instantly. Every hair on my body seemed as if it were standing straight up from the kinetic energy.

Donovan placed his hands on my shoulders and dug deeper. He felt so good, a tear slid down my face. He showed me no munificence as he gave it to me. Just when I thought I was going to go crazy from the wild fucking, he led me to the bathroom.

"Put your hands on the counter."

I put my hands on the counter, he climbed back inside of me from behind, and gave my thick flesh a pounding again. I looked up into the mirror to take a look at his sex face. He was concentrating with his eyebrows nearly touching and biting on his lower lip. My hubby looked so sexy.

When he noticed I was staring through the mirror, he said, "That's right. Look at me."

Moaning loudly, my voice echoed off the acoustics of the bathroom's walls. His dick got harder and so did his strokes as he fucked me senseless. My moan then turned into a scream up to the heavens. That really got him going. As sweat dripped down his face, he exploded.

We were both out of breath as I collapsed against the bathroom counter. He leaned up against the wall and stared at me through the mirror. "See, what you did to me."

I laughed at him, wiped my sweaty face with my hands, turned around to face him, and replied, "Maybe I should've told you a long time ago, if I knew you'd fuck me that way."

He laughed and had a smile so big, it was hard for him to make it go away. "Wow..."

I walked over to the shower. "Will you be able to do that again?"

"Yeah...show me how you hold that gun again."

Le Boudoir

By

Lorraine Elzia

My toes clinch and then extend as I try to relax. Removing my shoes has always been the first thing I do once I get on an airplane. I'm not exactly sure where I got the idea from, but it has become an obsessive, compulsive, ritual of mine in order to calm my fear of flying. Hell, I'll try just about anything, at least once, to get the flying monkey off my back; and so far relaxing my feet is the only thing that seems to work for me. As I stare at my vulnerable, slightly exposed feet and begin to exhale through my flying anxieties, my attention is instantly diverted by a pair of midnight blue, form fitting, United Air-issued trousers.

Welcome to the friendly skies, I whisper to myself as my eyes become glued and start darting side to side down the aisle in the same rhythm as the ample ass of a sashaying flight attendant who whisks by me.

Carmella, reads her name tag; Ms. Jackson if you nasty; is what my mind perceives.

Uncontrollably, I begin to gyrate in my seat to the steady and provocative tempo of her hips. I instantly envision bending her over one of the passenger seats and testing out her floatation devices as I take her from behind. Trying to contain myself, I struggle not to think how it would feel if I rammed my cock into her nice juicy pussy.

Now that's a "Controlled" tight space I'd love to invade.

The thought crosses my mind as I try to inconspicuously grab between my legs in hopes of straightening out the crouching tiger that is ready to pounce on a very delectable prey. The lonely nights of being an "ex" have made it harder and harder, literally, to tame my manhood. Not having a nightly outlet for sex has given my Jimmy a mind of its own; and an increasing desire to announce its presence at will, between the warm, inviting lower folds in the midst of a woman's thighs.

Down boy, I hear the Mile High Club is truly overrated. The unconvincing caveat floats through my head; both of them—neither will listen.

I argue mentally with my erection and find a way to maintain my composure through Carmella's illustrations of what to do in case of an emergency. I have an emergency of my own developing in my pants, but I curtail it for the sake of the other passengers.

Love at first sight is an ideal I do not believe in; instead I am what you might call a groupie to lust being medicine for the soul. The uncontrollable aching of my third leg signifies my approval that Ms. United Air has just what the doctor ordered to refill my sexual prescription any time, any place. My fingers rub across my temples. I shift in my seat. At least wait till we land, my mind scolds again. This time both heads listen and I comply.

Fresh off the heels of an ugly divorce via Anna Marie and her legal entourage, I have developed a blind eye to the prospect of love. Battered, bruised and sucker punched by Cupid's arrow, I quickly learned the lessons from my emotional scars which had dug their way deep into my psyche. Never again will I be a victim of love; but lust on the other hand, well, that Harlot still has a home in my heart and I have to evict her ass from time to time.

I had married for the old-fashion reason—love; but that bitch of a dog had bitten me so hard in the ass so many times that I swore never to feel the wrath of her teeth again. The old adage of "Love conquering all" had never crossed paths with the likes of Anna Marie.

A poster child for ruthlessness, Anna Marie was heartless when it came to torturing the soul; and even more so when it came to leaving casualties of war. She loved stepping over dead bodies on her path to self-fulfillment. From the moment I first met her and laid eyes on that mesmerizing hour-glass figure of hers, she had taken my breath away. She was my oxygen; my world. Parts of me were embarrassed concerning the things I had done in the name of love—for her. I was a slave to Anna Marie, inside and out. My greatest pleasure on earth was the time spent running my tongue up and down every crevice of her delectable body. The rich, succulent, flavor of her flesh had a way of somehow sullying, by comparison, the satisfaction of even the most exquisite chocolate truffle. The taste of her skin on the palate of my mouth was something I lived for. But I never should have married her. I never should have fallen in love. I should have just fucked her; over and over again...real good; and then just kept it moving.

Gone are the nights of hitting the headboard so hard

against the wall that the pictures fell off and the lamps hit the floor from being shaken from their perch on their respective night stands. Seven years, and episode after episode of degrading later, Anna Marie has stolen not only my taste buds, my heart and my soul; but all of my material goods as well.

It was Anna Marie's ability to sniff out a dime even if it was buried six feet underground that had brought me to the Louisiana Bayou. Her need to squeeze out every single drop of her self-proclaimed portion of everything I owned, was the fire that helped her find out that I had property in the Bayou that even I was clueless about.

My great, great aunt Henrietta Banks had left the Banks Estate to me, her only living relative, in her will. Legal bureaucracy and red tape upon her death were aides in ensuring that the paper trail of ownership of the property never seemed to make its way back to me personally. I had no clue Henrietta existed, that she had died, or that I was her only heir to her estate. No harm, no foul. You can't miss something or someone you've never had or known. Ignorance was bliss in my case. That is until Anna Marie decided she was entitled to half of everything that was mine, including, but not limited to the Banks Estate.

Before I would willingly give away half of my family's legacy, even one I never knew existed, I thought it would be wise to take a look at it first to see if I should include my new-found property in the New Orleans Plantation Country under the umbrella of the white flag of surrender to my ex-wife; or if I should battle over it with Anna Marie in court.

With the reminder of my priorities back in focus, Ms. Phat Ass United Air was put on the backburner of my thoughts as I try to mentally prepare for my Bayou destination.

Even the air inside the airport is sweltering to me as I

step off the plane and head towards the baggage claim area. As I struggle to become accustomed to the unfamiliar, thin, humid air pulsating through my lungs, I see her.

Her hands hold a single, small white sign. It is the second thing I notice when coming within fifty feet of her presence. Bold, black letters read, Julian Banks—nothing more; and nothing more is needed as an introduction between the two of us to our destiny.

The sign indicates that she is responsible for picking me up; her body language indicates the same thing, but for different reasons. A trail of unbridled sweat make its journey slowly down my back as I remove my coat jacket, mid-stride, and approach her.

Work the swagger baby, work the swagger. My mental coach directed each of my steps and I was obedient in motion.

The closer I get to her, the more pronounced become the fragrances of lavender, jasmine and saddle wood. It is a sensual aroma that, coupled with a gorgeous smile nestled within full, pouty lips, has a way of making all the florescent lights in the place seem dull; while making me become slightly aroused once again.

Down boy. Down! Comes the chastation once again from my mind.

"Mr. Banks? Julian Banks?" A smile that couldn't possibly get wider or brighter somehow does. I am a hostage to the deep dimple on the left side of her cheek that is a roommate to the sexiest mole I have ever seen in my life.

Her beauty turns me into a mute. Momentarily I lose the ability to think, let alone speak.

"Are you Mr. Julian Banks?" Her words, to no avail, try to coax me back into focus.

"I am Geneive. Unless you have an objection, I will be

your tour guide and show you to the Bank's Estate."

The way her name, and every other word, rolls off of her lips makes me instantly jealous of inanimate objects. Words are no longer words. They are skilled competitors in my mind for her attention and affection. I envy them for having the privilege to glide across her tongue.

Thick, but sensual is the accent that utters the few words she speaks. I find myself immediately seduced as each innocent syllable hits the air and becomes a sadistic master with me as its slave.

Innocent. Even from the beginning I knew she was anything but.

"If I had of known I would be greeted by such a lovely sight, I would have freshened up a bit first before getting off the plane." I try to hold on to my inner Mack and subdue the fact that I am a bit off balance by being in her presence.

"Life is driven by pheromones Mr. Banks; never willingly extinguish yours. Your efforts to do so are unnatural to who you are and they only defy the laws of attraction."

Who says shit like that on a first meeting? Intrigue...thy real name is Geneive, is all my mind can muster.

"Hummm, that's an interesting way to look at things." I move in closer, hoping that my natural scent is truly as appealing to her as she has implied.

"This is your first time in the Bayou, isn't it Mr. Banks? You will learn, all too quickly, that everything and everyone here believes in the laws of nature. It is more than a creed of ours, it is our gospel. Playing with nature is sacrilegious to us. Therefore we resist the temptation of playing a game we know we will lose. Are you a winner Mr. Banks?" The indention of her dimple seems to sink in a little further and so does my desire to know the woman behind it.

"I would like to think I am." I respond.

"Well then, never fight nature. It's smarter than any of us will ever be."

The air around her suffocates me in a surprisingly enjoyable way. Long, spiral curls fall in front of her face as her head moves side to side as she speaks. I watch, in slow motion, as she brushes ringlet after ringlet from side to side. It is almost as if her beautiful mane, which seems to have a mind of its own in drifting into her line of vision, is an annoyance to her.

Her irritant trash is my new-found guilty treasure.

The removal of her hair from its original position of covering her eyes and the oval frame of her face, gives me an even clearer view of her outer beauty and a deeper appreciation for the creation of all women of color. God really was showing off when He made her. She is more than a Nubian Princess. At this very moment in time, she is my Bayou Queen and everything about her is regal; at least in my eyes.

Within her high cheek bones and exotic slanted eyes lies the magnificent splendor that only God Almighty could think to create in the form of a Creole woman of color. It was an unselfish act on His part to share something so beautiful with the rest of us unworthy creatures. Her skin is flawless as if it has been air-brushed by God's hands and kissed by Mother Nature. I can't help myself from pausing and taking in every inch of her beauty until my mind is full to the point of mental, if not physical, gratification. Truth be told, just looking at her walks a thin line of fulfilling both—mental and physical—with very little effort on her part. Her essence alone is enough to satisfy most wants and desires even before a touch is given.

"Forgive my ignorance; what is your name again?"

"Geneive." She responds as she places her arm around

mine and walks towards the turnstile to help me retrieve my luggage. Suddenly a three-syllable word takes on an eternity of its own simply by the manner in which it is spoken.

Geneive. Geneive. Geneive. God damn, her name is ALMOST as sexy as she is. I think to myself. I feel my nuts get tighter just from the way her lips move to say her own name.

"It means, 'Woman of the people', she says with a prideful arrogance that I can't help but love and admire. The bitch is sexy, even without trying.

"Do you live up to your namesake?" I ask as I lick my lips slowly, but seductively, to ensure that she knows that two can play her game. A true Mack senses game; even in female form.

"At each and every chance I am given and even the ones I choose to create on my own." Geneive replies.

Her confidence draws me deeper into her than I am comfortable admitting.

"But that's not the reason for your trip. Allow me to be your tour guide for the basis of why you are here in the Bayou. I'll show you the sites, Monsieur Banks, that you came here for. Anything else you gain along your journey will just be a bonus attraction. Consider it 'free' of charge."

Geneive winks with her last statement. Both my mind and my dick skip a beat at the possibilities of what bonuses she might have that I might receive.

Let me state, for the record that I am confident in the fact that I know I am what most ladies would consider a good catch. I've read the books and watched the TV shows, so I know that a lot of women say that a good black man is hard to find.

I am among what some women label as a dying breed. The single black man that is straight, not in jail, has a job, looks good, is God fearing, lays massive pipe with skill, isn't full of himself and knows how to treat a woman.

I work hard at trying to be anything but a stereotypical male. I do my best to give a new definition to taking care of myself. Words like; "metro sexual," "bougie," or a "high maintenance man" never deter my need or desire to look good for the opposite sex. I have high standards for myself. I like looking good and smelling good for both myself, as well as for women. Real men do that. We don't let what others say or do dictate our stride. We do what we do because we like doing it; regardless to the opinions of others. We are who we are. I am who I am. I make no apologies for catering to my outside appearance or for wanting to turn a head or two when I enter a room. I might not be willing to try and get back on the horse of falling in love again; but I am always willing to try to get a piece of ass on the whim of two willing parties; myself being one of them.

I have been told that I am handsome, distinguished and a real gentleman. I recognize what it takes to be both pleasing in my own eyes, as well as those of the opposite sex. I aim to please both—me, and any potential mate I may find along the way. I don't think there is anything wrong with that line of thinking. More men should embrace it and more women should appreciate it. Anna Marie may not have valued my efforts; but she was just one fish. There are many others out there in the sea of life. Her apprehension to being hooked on the line of my love never lessened my craving for throwing out my rod and reel into the ocean to see what other fish would take the bait at the end of my pole.

"Our journey to your estate will be a short one Mr. Banks. It is only..."

"Julian. Please call me Julian." I interrupt her because I simply want to hear how my name sounds coming from her lips.

"Alright...Julian it is." She smiles and tucks her hair behind her ears on both sides. Just as anticipated, I love how my name sounds delivered through her sexy accent. She can say my name over and over and I would be in heaven each time she does. If I can get her to scream it in the throes of passion...I would die a happy man.

"Our driver will take us to the Bank's Estate and once we are there, I will give you a short tour of the place. We can go into all of the other details more tomorrow. Today will just be an appetizer. Tomorrow is your full course meal of the entire place. But for now...just follow me."

Little does Geneive know that her ability to make my pole rise on command, without touch, gives her a lust-filled control over me. She has the added ability to override my brain; so much so, that I would follow her to the ends of the Earth.

As promised, our ride is short but scenic. Sunlight filters through the lush green trees along the banks of the Sabine River to our final destination. In the midst of visions of swampy marsh, I can't help but notice alligators scampering to dry land and pelicans sunning themselves on floating logs. Geneive narrates my surroundings and I pretend to listen. As she educates me, in detail, on the French history of the area and the lineage of Creole ancestry that has taken care of my family's estate for centuries, I can't help but watch the rise and fall of her breasts which seem to be speaking to me as well. She speaks of heritage, honor, and the decline of the plantation over the years. My ears hear everything she has to say, but my mind wanders—giving only her perky breasts the true dedication they desire and deserve. Suddenly I have an interest only in matters that revolve around the tasting of her skin. Nothing more.

She wears a short summer dress; lilac in color. It is

tight around her breasts and flows freely along the hem. Thin spaghetti straps support her muscular, but feminine arms. She sits close to me and her body language is open and forgiving which causes me to reciprocate the same vibe unto her. Her left leg is crossed over her right ,with her knees touching mine; a position that causes a feeling of familiar comfortableness which hugs me all over. My nature begins to rise to full attention.

"Louisiana summers always bring with them an unbearable likeness of being." Geneive leans in and whispers in my ear.

"Pardon me? What does that mean?"

'You're staring at your surroundings, both inside and out of this car, and suddenly things that didn't make sense to you before now are starting to make sense, if only vaguely. You have a sense of Déjà vu." She stares out the window, void of eye contact, while my eyes continue their contact with her breasts.

"How do you do that?" I ask as I begin to accept how true her statement seems in relation to my current existence.

"Do what?"

"Read my mind—sense my spirit. How do you do that?"

"It's not magic Julian. You wear your feelings on your chest and you're wide open to a woman like me. I can sense your needs. It's part of being a woman. We can feel these things when we choose to pay attention to our ability. It's Nature's gift to us. It's in our genetic makeup; it just takes a special connection within our inner selves to be able to give it life."

I notice her sizing me up from head to toe and I welcome her intrusive eyes. I find myself lying back in my seat, hoping that her hands will take the same path that her eyes do—starting at my clean-shaven bald head with a caress, and ending at my dick with a stroke or two. Crossed legs seem to lose some of their rigidity as she rubs them against mine. I pray under my breath that more will follow. If I didn't know any better, I would swear that the mole on her left calf somehow winks at me, inviting me to touch it.

"A real woman knows how to make a man feel like a man. Like the king he is. It's a mixture of giving him submissiveness when that is what he wants and controlling him when he wants to be controlled. A man has two sides to his nature. He has a Doppelganger; we all do. Sometimes he wants to lead and other times he wants to be lead. A real woman gives a man what he wants."

"And being a Woman of the People helps you know all of that?" I shift in my seat to relieve built-up sexual tension.

"Well, it certainly doesn't hurt. I was given the name because my destiny was set at my birth. I just follow its path."

Her nipples seem to get harder with our conversation, or maybe that is just my wishful thinking. Whatever the case, I can't help but enjoy the way her ample breast move side to side through the braless constraint that tries to contain them.

I know I shouldn't be daydreaming about mixing business with pleasure, but sometimes common sense is overshadowed by the call of the wild. This is one of those times.

We arrived at the estate and I can't hide my disappointment. It is grand in size, but years of neglect have taken its toll on a place that I can only imagine must have been magnificent back in its prime. As Geneive takes me on a guided tour of the big house of the Banks Estate, I do a mental check of the aura around me, ensuring that there is still a certain confidence behind my swagger.

Outwardly I feign interest in the raised basement, the

servant quarters, the gallery, grounds and the wine cellar; inwardly my mind struggles hard to keep my eyes off of Geneive's ass.

"What's that over there?" I point out the window, past the weathered pool, to a small set of three, small, pre-fabricated buildings on the south side of the house.

"Those are boudoirs, but only one is still in use. None of the workers stay on the property anymore except me. When I am not taking care of the main house, I stay in one of the boudoirs."

"Boudoir? Is that like a guest house or something?" I ask the question as my eyes dart to the rest of the entryway to the house.

Geneive lowers her head and chuckles slightly, as she proceeds to pour me a drink.

"Something like that Julian. Actually it is a little more than that. If I need a place just to live, the Banks Estate has ample room enough for that and I do have a space here that I call home. A boudoir is more like a lady's private room; a space for leisure, enjoyment, entertainment and relaxation. And for some women, Le Boudoir is her spot in the universe which houses all aspects of her personality—free of inhibition."

"Sounds intriguing. Is your boudoir part of the full-course meal portion of my tour for tomorrow?" I say as I sip on the glass of warm brandy she has given me.

"It's your property Julian. Your birthright. I own no portion of that. But my boudoir is a part of that 'bonus' I spoke of."

"Touché Geneive. Touché."

She abruptly ends our conversation and shows me to my room. It is back to business with Geneive giving me instructions on the house and advising me that a meal has been prepared for me for the night. She also states that everyone else has gone home already for the evening, but that they will return in the morning.

"I have started the ceiling fans to give you some circulation, but the night can be unforgiving in its heat. A shower and a few more drinks should help you feel a little bit more comfortable, and should also help you make it through the night."

Geneive refreshes my glass with more brandy and a few more cubes of ice. Then just as simply as she had introduced herself at the airport, she leaves in the same manner.

I stare around the master suite trying to become accustomed to my surroundings. Portraits of Banks family members, resting on chaise lounge chairs provocatively dressed, if dressed at all, aligned each of the walls. Some of the portraits are visions I could have gone my whole life without having their sights swimming around in my head. Each is beautifully done, exposing a talent that could only be compared to some of the greatest artists recognized by man. But some images of family members, no matter how tastefully done, should not be shared with others in the same bloodline.

I decide to wash off the sweat building up on my body and to take a look around the rest of the house. The halls are dark; with small oil lamps strategically place to give just enough light to illuminate my path. The sounds of crickets, owls, croaking lizards and other creatures of the night are my only companions along my journey; besides my new glass of brandy.

There is a certain kind of peacefulness lurking in the halls as I move room to room on a treasure hunt through my family's past. I can't believe the size of the house, or the fact that it is a piece of property that actually belongs to me. The thought is overwhelming as I begin to worry that I will get lost and be unable to find my way back to my room in the middle of the night.

For a brief moment, being alone in an unfamiliar place gets the best of me. Seeking solace by way of the moon beams peeking inside the windows, I stop and stare out of one of them on to the grounds of the estate. The night is clear and in the distance I see a flicker of lights coming from the boudoirs.

Geneive. I think and can't help but smile.

Lascivious thoughts of what might be going on within the walls of her tiny boudoir bombard my mind. Curiosity gets the best of me. I venture outside the temporary comfort of unfamiliar walls.

I've got to know what she does down there in that dirty little secret of hers. I think to myself as I find the way to the door with my horniness tugging at my mind.

A blast of night heat hits me as I begin walking the worn path to her building. I have no clue what I expect to find there, or even what I will say to her once I arrive; but I am drawn to the boudoir and its contents like a moth to a flame. As I get closer, I can see her walking back and forth inside; gathering small items and placing them on a pedestal. She has on a red satin robe drawn loosely in the front. She appears to be naked underneath. Her breasts sing, "hello, look at me" through the opening in the front and I long to give them my own saliva-filled salutation in response. Instead, I stand on the small porch in utter darkness—peering through her window—contemplating my next move.

"Voyeurism is against the law here in the Bayou; that is unless you ask permission first. Are you going to stand out there watching me all night, or do you plan on coming in?" Geneive's voice, spoken through the open window, startles me before I have a chance to knock.

"While I do like to watch every now and then, I insist in only dealing with willing parties to any game I play. I was actually planning on asking if I could come in. You just beat me to the punch. Something you have been doing since I got here. How did you know I was out here?"

"I could smell you before you even arrived. There haven't been any new men around here in years. Your warm, male scent came down the hill long before you did. It's inviting, recognizable, and undeniable to me now. Thank you for taking my advice and not fighting against your pheromones or your nature; both of which brought you down the hill here to me."

She opens the door and takes my glass out of my hand, turning her back to me. I smile as I watch her robe get captured then released and captured then released into the crack of her ass as she walks.

"Make yourself at home. At least for now." She invites.

Geneive walks over to a small table where several bottles of wine, fine liquors, and other odd-shaped bottles with liquids in them reside. Placing a single cube of ice in her glass and then in mine, she takes a third cube and slowly runs it along her forehead, temples, neck and ultimately down the front of her robe before allowing it to disappear in her mouth. Her lips pucker as her mouth plays seductively with her frozen treat.

"So this is where all the magic happens?" I say as I take my glass from her and sip its content while taking a seat on a small couch in the corner of the room.

"What kind of magic are you expecting to happen here Julian?"

Her tone is condescending yet curious in manner. She sits down next to me, one leg crossed under the other. A nipple winking at me. Her fingertips run down the side of my face and

I close my eyes, going along with her seductive flow. Having her so close to me makes the temperature in the room rise even more. Experienced fingertips dance seductively along my eyebrows and softly over my eyelashes before traveling down to my mustache and goatee. One finger lingers along my lips as she remarks how succulent they are.

"Supple and smooth, begging to be kissed." She whispers as she continues to run a trail down my jawline.

"I'm not sure what I was expecting Geneive. Maybe I had some Louisiana voodoo magic in mind, I suppose. But I must say, I can see why you prefer this place to the main house."

The room screams sex all around me. It was created, if not designed, for lust. Quaint in nature and soothing in comfort, I feel mesmerized by its allure. Several mysterious pendants and wind chimes hang from different spots in the room. Small porcelain dishes house what I perceive to be roots, powdery substances and pieces of dried berries. She must use those for her black-magic potions, my superstitious mind perceives. I chuckle out loud at my thoughts. Red velvet curtains and exotic abstract paintings cover the walls; most are images of half-naked men and women in various positions. There are no real lights in the room, only about ten or fifteen large candles which fill the air with a hazelnut fragrance that gives an ambiance to the room unlike anything I have experienced before. As the candle flames flicker, they make it at least ten degrees hotter in the room than it needs to be on an already hot night.

"After a while you get used to it." She says, guided by devious intentions of her own. She begins to pull my sweat-drenched T-shirt over my head, ignoring my voodoo reference.

My limbs are limp and I oblige like the puppet she wants me to be.

"Get used to what?" I ask.

"The heat."

She continues to run her hands slowly down my chest while gyrating her body next to mine to the rising crescendo of the music playing in the background. Her movements signify she is in the midst of some hypnotic, self-induced foreplay. I feel honored to be able to watch and be a participant to her show.

Her movements are thorough and deliberate. Almost as if she is examining me with both her hands and her hips. Sharp nails run down my torso. Goose bumps form. I tighten my chest muscles allowing her to indulge in the rock hardness of my upper torso that hours in the gym have produced. As if she can read my mind, Geneive begins massaging my neck and slowly rubbing my bald head. Her actions seem to give her as much pleasure as they give me in the form of relaxation. She does not say the words, but I swear I hear them through her unmoving lips.

I'm going to fuck the shit out of you. They say. Or at least that is what I hear.

Slowly she stands up from beside me and positions herself so that she is straddling over my lap. Her body is hot, soaked in sweat. She maintains direct eye contact with me, never losing a visual grasp of connection as she lowers herself over my rock-hard cock; continuing to examine my body with her hands.

I am under the spell of her smile and I make sure I don't release my eye contact with her either. Eye to eye we remain as she grinds on my lap. We are locked in a concentration that supersedes what our bodies are doing. The sounds of the night seem to sing along with the sultry jazz that is playing in the background. I feel my manhood swell several inches in appreciation during the time it takes for her hands to move from caressing my chest and arms, to making their way down to the top of my jogging pants.

Any attempts to try and act like I have control over my dick are futile and have flown out the window along with any 'getting to know you jitters" I might have had concerning Geneive. My dick is begging to come out and play with the grown folks.

"It's a shame to leave him all tied up like that." She says as she rubs aggressively through my pants on my dick. "Why don't you take these off and let him out?" She squeezes real hard on my growing cock. Geneive leans back, plants a kiss on my groin area and then slowly rises up off of my lap. As she, does so, her robe opens, ever so slightly, and I catch a glimpse of a tattoo on her left breast, which glistens in her perspiration. I long to see the rest of it and hear the history behind how and why it got there.

"It really does not seem fair for me to be naked all alone." I say as I stand up and began removing my jogging pants.

"You won't be. At least not for long. What fun would there be in that? Come sit over here."

She watches me through wavy strands of honey-brown hair. A few strands seem to have escaped from the clasp that was supposed to hold them captive. She motions toward a tan-colored chaise lounge and turns on one of the few lamps in the room. With precision she moves the light so that it points directly on to the lounge chair. My eyes adjust to the light and to her beautifully exposed body as she unties her robe, allowing it to fall to the floor.

Gracefully she moves towards me. Her hands are gentle as she positions me on the chaise in the exact manner she desires. Her silhouette in motion is breathtaking. She instructs me to lay on my left side in a supine position with my upper torso elevated slightly.

I do as I am told while watching her stand before me naked with one hand on her hip and one hand on her lip— deep in thought. With tenderness she runs her hands up and down my thighs and then along the sides of my shaft making sure my erection is just right. Exactly like she likes it. For a few moments she steps back to her original position and just stares.

She returns to me and sits down on the chaise, then she leans in with her hands raised above me to adjust the pillows behind my head. Her right breast caresses my lips haphazardly as it hangs over my head during her pillow mission. I resist the urge to take it entirely into my mouth, but I lick my lips once it is out of reach.

"I get a little carried away with trying to create the perfect moment. Next to our memories, sometimes only a painting will do in capturing a moment. Remember Julian...within these walls there are no inhibitions. Please just sit still and both of us will let nature take its course."

"Tell me the story behind your tattoo." I try to feel more comfortable as she fusses with the lamp in the room to make sure it shines on me in the right manner.

"It is an image of Gaia, the Greek goddess of the Earth. There is no story behind my getting it other than she was whole and complete in herself, and so am I."

The way she ends her statement indicates that is all she is going to say about it, so I leave the matter alone. Starring at the tattoo would be as close to that mystery as I was going to get.

I watch as she walks to a small stool in front of a pedestal in the center of the room. Beads of sweat trickle down her forehead and I can see small pellets between her cleavage as well. Neither deter her from her mission at hand.

There is a certain sexual vulnerability in allowing another person to create a portrait of you. I sit perfectly still as I am instructed to do. Geneive has a way of dominating not only my mind, but my body as well with simple eye moments and pure sexual will. Mentally I hate myself for being such a willing slave. Physically I welcome—no NEED—to relinquish myself, through submission, to her commands. Sheer anticipation of the treats she will surrender unto me for my good behavior are motivation enough for me to do as I am told.

"Keep it hard, but not too hard." She whispers as I watch her hands make whimsical, but flowing, caresses from her brush. I mimic her strokes on the canvas with my own strokes to my erection. Slowly, yet precisely; just as I see her do with her brush. Good foreplay can't be rush; neither can seduction if it is done right. Geneive taught me that. Life imitates art; and I am the star pupil in her class.

Hues of brown and black paint flicker freely into the sultry air inside her boudoir as the heat of the night begins to drench my entire body. I'll admit it. I love the sticky feeling enveloping me and the sweaty smell emanating from both our bodies. The aroma of anticipated lust can be intoxicating; and I am becoming drunk in the moment.

Her legs seem to have a mind of their own in uncontrollably spreading wider and wider as she becomes spellbound in her mission of immortalizing me through portrait. In between my strokes up and down and down and up, I stare. I admire. I long to be inside the warmth that resides between her sugary thighs.

"You keep a well-trimmed garden; just like I like it." I manage to say without breaking my rhythm or hers.

She bites her bottom lip while concentrating on getting the perfect movement of the brush to capture my manhood; our eyes dance in unison of lovemaking that only two naked bodies admiring one another can do—without touch.

"The garden is the entrance to other pleasures. It is a representation of what lies inside." She continues painting without missing a beat.

Geneive manages to speak between glancing back and forth between my crotch and her canvass. Fluidity dictates her movements, guiding her right hand to paint while her left hand shifts between kneading her titty nipples and fingering her pussy. I watch as she rubs fiercely at her clit with her index finger and thumb, while inserting her middle finger in and out of her snatch. As her juices build and begin to drip, occasionally she captures her own wetness on her fingertip and flings it carelessly on to the canvass as if it is a secret sauce or ingredient essential to the painting.

That shit was nasty, but watching it turned me on immensely. An image overtakes my mind of bending her over the pedestal that held her paint and brushes, and taking her from behind while her pussy maintains a death grip on my dick. But it remains nothing more than an image that helps me maintain my erection.

Intensely and rapidly she moves through the painting as if her strokes are guided by a cadence other than her own. A sparkle of desire seems to shine through her eyes and I feel her devouring me visually—inch by inch. I continue to stroke myself and she continues to watch and paint.

The velocity of her strokes begin to slow down and that is my signal that her painting is almost complete. All I can hope for is that she will not let my good erection go to waste. I've been a good boy. I deserve a treat. She makes a bold movement in the bottom right-hand corner of the canvass just as the clock on the wall begins to chime twelve times to signify that the bewitching hour is upon us. She glances at the clock. Midnight. The time for lovers.

Almost as if on cue, a more dominate side of Geneive emerges.

"You know you have been sexually harassing my mind all day." She says boldly.

Her spontaneous admission catches me off guard. I know that I've been contemplating our bodies dancing horizontally together since the moment I saw her in the airport. But until this very moment, I've been guessing as to if the feeling was mutual, or if Geneive was merely messing with my head.

"They say you cannot harass the 'willing'."

"Is that what 'they' say?" She giggles while walking towards me.

Falling to her knees, she crawls the last few feet that exist between us. My only regret is that I am not viewing her actions from behind; getting a bird's-eye view of her hole drooling in a wetness running down her pussy on display while on all fours.

"It's beautiful out here. Hot, but beautiful. There is a reason we are here together Geneive. We may not know why right now; but we are meant to be together, right here, right now, under this moon and in the heat of this night." I keep my eyes glued on hers as she slowly crawls seductively towards me.

Her fingers start at my toes. I've never had a foot fetish and never knew a woman that had one either. The attention she gives to my feet before placing my toe in her mouth is foreign to me; but the feeling is nothing short of pure ecstasy. She follows my toe job with a massage that extends throughout my whole body. Tingles invade my spine and lust-filled goose bumps cover my skin. Her tongue follows her fingers, canvassing my core.

Soon there is flesh on flesh.

I let out a moan.

"Did you know that some people believe that the real strength of a man resides in his dick. It holds not only the power to bring forth life, but also stores all of his inner strength."

She grasps my dick with both of her hands, working them simultaneously as she moves my hand out of her way to ensure that the job is done right.

"If you keep touching me that way, you are going to experience all of my strength first hand." I manage to say through my pants of pleasure.

"Is that a promise?" She runs her tongue up and down my shaft. I shift on the chair, removing one of the pillows from behind my head in order to get more comfortable.

"No promises Geneive...only guarantees."

I allow my hands to touch her body for the first time. They thank me for the gift and the opportunity.

Geneive's head motion goes in sync with her lip sucking motion. Like a pro, she takes in all nine inches that I possess. Appreciative of my manly blessing. She doesn't neglect my balls; they feel the warm of her mouth as well. I watch the rise and fall of her cheeks and guide her head with my hands; ensuring my stick hits the back of her throat with each thrust. Between sucks, she runs circles around my shaft with her tongue and makes butterfly movements on the mushroom head.

"Damn girl. That feels so good." I moan while allowing my eyes to roll back in my head.

"Hush. I didn't tell you to speak." She admonishes me

while taking in every drop I have, leaving a connecting line of saliva from her lips to my dick's tip. In much the same manner as a starving person would devour a morsel of bread, Geneive hungrily slobs on my knob as if it is the last dick on the face of the planet and she is a sexually-famished vagabond. I'm just grateful that I can help feed the hungry.

I feel the come building inside of me; on the point of eruption. I know I can't hold on to it for too much longer.

"Don't you dare!" She warns as if reading my mind that my time is coming. "Not yet!"

Geneive moves in closer. Nipples hard and standing up, she takes my rock hard dick in one hand and places it between her breasts, pushing them together. Size 40 D's provide a source of warmth and soft friction that makes my toes slowly begin to curl. Skillfully she uses one hand to hold both her breasts in place around my shaft; with the other she rubs her fingers up and down the exposed portion of my dick and with her tongue she performs a lapping motion on the tip—sucking up the pre-cum that has formed. It's a three-punch power play to my dick that I love. The rubbing motion of both of her hands, coupled with the licking of her tongue is more than my dick can handle. I've suppressed exploding longer than humanly possible. I hear myself grunting loud and fast before I even know that I am shooting my load.

"That's it baby. Give it all to me." Geneive murmurs as she closes her eyes while I release my come.

I continue to pump between her breasts forcefully, depleting my balls of all of the fluid inside them.

"Nothing beats a good cum shot." Geneive remarks, licking her lips while smiling up at me.

My breathing is heavy. My heart pace fast. The signs of a great orgasm are all over me.

"Don't get too comfortable just yet. We aren't done." Geneive begins to slither up my body; rubbing her skin against mine every step of the way.

"It's time for you to show me the real source of your strength. I've been waiting all day for you to give me what we French call, 'La Petite Mort'." Her accent makes a phrase that I don't understand sound surprisingly desirable.

"What is that?" Labored breathing precedes my question.

"It means, 'little death'...our description of an orgasm." She reclines on her back working her breasts again with one hand and darting her fingers in and out of her well-trimmed garden with the other. I can't help but grin unrepentantly at her.

I watch as she works herself into a heated frenzy. As she plays with herself I can see that her clit is soaked from her self-arousal. My mind is willing to join her, but after more than an hour of suppressing my own orgasm, my body is not a willing participant.

Sensing my need for more of a stimulant, Geneive walks over to one of the porcelain dishes and sprinkles some of its powdery substance into a fresh glass and pours me a drink.

"This will make for a good night for both of us," she says as she hands the drink in my direction.

"What's in it?" I ask, skeptical to drink its contents.

"Let's just say it's some of that 'black magic' you came here searching for." She smiles and takes a sip of my drink first to let me know it is safe.

I follow her lead like I had done for most of the day. Immediately I feel the blood rushing to my dick causing it to rise. A smile takes control of Geneive's face and she instantly and willingly bends over the side of the chaise lounge.

"Take it slow at first. When I want you to go faster, I will tell you. And if I'm not moaning...you ain't doing it right. Start over!"

I place my hands on each of her butt cheeks, spreading them wider in order to get a full look at her treasure box. The plumpness of her pussy lips calls for me to suck them. An uncontrollable craving for pussy juice on my lips vetoes my dick's ability to go first in tasting her. I want to lick it before I stick it.

"Mangez-moi! Mangez-moi maintenant!" She whispers. Eat me! Eat me now!

I oblige.

I start off slow just as she told me to. Long strokes of my tongue start below her belly, near the top of her vagina and go in an upward motion towards her ass hole which is raised in the air. I hear the first moan from deep within her gut.

I know I am doing it right.

Shifting between licks and sucks, I occasionally insert a finger or two deep inside her and watch them work with concise precision. Her ass, as well as her inner thighs, begin to quiver with each thrust that my tongue delivers.

She moans again.

Longer this time.

I dig deeper and deeper with my fingers watching them disappear within her walls. A slippery substance oozes from between her legs and begins to cover not only my fingers, but my whole hand. Soon well-manicured fingertips spread her lower lips apart as Geneive takes it upon herself to clear a path for my tongue; relieving my fingers and ordering my tongue to return to its duty station. I suck with a ferocity that causes my jaws to ache.

Geneive lets out her first scream of the night.

She rolls over on her back. One leg is raised on the back

of the lounge chair as she rubs her pussy.

"We're still not done yet. Come here." She uses her finger to beacon me towards her. Slowly I start tasting her flesh. From the inside of her knees, up her inner thighs to her belly button. Her back arches, pushing her breasts forward in a manner that begs me to place them in my mouth.

"The only thing better than a titty fuck is a titty I can suck." I say before my lips come into contact with her left nipple. Its surface is saturated with chill bumps of pleasure. As I bite gently around the dark portion of her perky and protruding titties, I can't help but be thankful that she has more than a hand or mouthful of satisfaction for me to indulge in.

It's as if a jolt of electric pleasure has made her nipples so hard that she could break glass with them. The goose bumps on her breasts speak to me in a braille form of pleasure. My fingers and tongue read them as a signal to continue what I am doing. I release her breasts from my lips and begin kissing up the side of her neck, lingering at her ear lobes. I allow my tongue to dart in and out of her ear and exhale breaths of passion slowly into it as well. I can almost see the hair stand up on the back of her neck as she slowly begins to grin against the air between our bodies.

Her grinding tells me it's time.

I move to a standing position and place each of my hands on each of her legs; pushing them further apart.

Spread eagle is the position I need her in to do both of us justice.

My eyes connect with hers and then they direct her to watch me enter her garden.

This time she is the one doing the obliging.

Her eyes watch in anticipation as my soldier prepares for battle, finding his way into her gate without physical assistance. He's hard as a rock, at full attention, and long and strong in armor. I smile at her, maintaining eye contact knowing that I'm getting ready to give her the La Petite Mort that she asked for and then some.

From my first thrust I can feel her body instinctively begin to try to move away from me. She definitely isn't ready for how I intend to bring it. She underestimated me. That's for damn sure!

Take it slow at first, her words echo in my head and I intend to make her eat them. Seductive accent included. Slow is my specialty. Jack rabbit movements are for those in a hurry to get a nut; that is far from my intent. I enjoy savoring the moment. Just like good foreplay, good loving takes time.

I move as if on a mission. Deeper and deeper I penetrate her walls. Piercing are my strokes. She catches each and every thrust as if her life, instead of just an orgasm, depend on it. Her moans and groans become louder; ultimately turning into screams. I watch as she grabs into the air at shit that ain't there.

Time to shift gears. I quicken the pace just a little. Enough to raise the tone of her screams. I swear I can hear the animals in the area answering what they perceive to be a mating call. My hips dip with each push into her flesh. So thick, so thick, my mind chants as I watch the rise and fall of her hips to the rhythm I dictate and provide.

I can feel her pussy contracting like a clinched fist. I am pleased. So is she.

"Your dick is black magic. I love the way your one-eyed snake casts a spell on my body." Geneive states as she starts shaking uncontrollably.

I remove my hands from her legs and grab for her hands instead. I place each of my fingers on both of my hands in the spaces between hers. Our fingertips, eyes, and souls are intertwined for a moment in time.

My body begins to roll in a pattern of ecstasy that warns me that I am about to come. No longer am I in control. I quit fighting and let go to the point that my pending orgasm is about to suffocate me. I squeeze Geneive's fingers tightly as my breathing gets heavier and picks up pace. She squeezes my hands back as her screams of pleasure fill the air. Our mutual pleasure is on the edge of fruition. It only takes a few more pumps from me delivering all of my dick into her in a manner that she can handle, before we both collapse from a satisfying orgasm amidst sexual exhaustion.

Our bodies are drenched in sweat, the windows are fogged and at least four of the candles have burned out.

I continue to lay on top of Geneive until both of our breathing returns to normal. Once our vital signs reach healthy levels, I roll over on my back and my eyes begin to exam the room again. The portrait of me that Geneive had created earlier stares back at me. I can't help but think how remarkable it seems that she was able to somehow capture not just my likeness, but my soul as well within the confines of a canvass.

A breeze begins to float in the air through her open windows. It is the first one I've experienced since touching Louisiana soil. The wind chimes hanging from the ceiling of Geneive's boudoir all begin to chime at the same time in an orchestra of an approving melody to all that has taken place within its walls.

She's asleep.

I thought beauty never rested, but she proves me wrong.

Through the low murmur of a snore that emits from Geneive's sleeping body, I gather my clothes and walk towards the painting. We hadn't discussed if it belonged to me or to her; but I want to have a piece of her with me to make it through the night, so I take it.

The walk back up the worn path to the main house seems longer as I carry the painting in the moonlight. Somehow the trip back is not as lonely as the trip had been down to the boudoir. Most of the oil lamps inside the main house have burned out while I was gone; but I no longer need them. Guided by instinct, I find my way, in the dark, back to the master suite.

Reaching for the light switch, I fumble between trying to hold the large painting and finding the spot on the wall that will give life to darkness.

Once I find the switch, I hold the painting with both hands at arm's length in front of me. My eyes search for a spot in which to hang it.

Then I see it.

The one thing that makes it all make sense.

I stare at portrait after portrait of my ancestors, and then I stare at the portrait of my own.

They all have one thing in common.

A large marking in the lower right-hand corner.

It is her name.

Geneive.

Suddenly I know that I am not the first, nor will I be the last to experience the treasures that lie within the walls of Le Boudoir.

Far Away

By

LaLaina Knowles

Woke up for the second morning in a row with the same epiphany. I tossed around in bed, stared at the ceiling and eventually planted both feet on the ground in an attempt to start a day that seemed endless and I thought to myself, "I wish I didn't miss you so much".

As I did habitually daily, I powered on my laptop to prepare for another twelve-hour work day, of course not without visiting my favorite social network to update my status. Pondering on whether I would update my status to a funny quote or a message of inspiration, I realized I had received a poke. Life as I once knew it the day prior, forever changed in November 2011 with a friend request and a simple poke on a popular social media network. Sitting in disbelief deliberating on whether or not I should accept the request and possibly open up a chapter from my past that I may not have been prepared for, or perhaps write a story with a not so happy ending, I stared at the profile picture on the computer screen in a surreal state. I battled with several thoughts, including the thought that someone was surely playing a cruel joke that was hardly humorous; however, with much hesitation, I confirmed his friendship. The reasoning behind such doubt surfaced because a man that I have secretly wanted for over twenty-five years, a man I never thought I would see again, was no longer a figment of my imagination, he was real and attainable.

Over the years, I have often thought of Trey. Never in a sexual manner, simply wondering how life has treated him over the years; and those thoughts were often filled with other regrets and unanswered questions. The standard, "what ifs" that most people tend to replay in their heads after feeling as if they have missed out on a once-in-a-lifetime opportunity for true love. Knowing the chances of reconnecting with someone after going their separate ways was slim to none when you are hundreds of miles apart, especially with no direct contact for over two decades. Since I had last seen him, as a child, my life has taken me to many states and several counties; therefore, our chances of reconnecting was virtually impossible.

The way things began to unfold between myself and Trey, I was certain that this chance encounter was anything but chance; it was definitely fate. After encountering several challenges in my adult life with men, would this be another meaningless encounter? Or could this be the beginning of something beautiful? Although I wasn't certain how things would turn out between the two of us, I was certain that I was prepared to uncover all there was to discover about this man. My six year on-and-off relationship with Durrell had finally run its course with him being emotionally unavailable and commitment phobic. Not to mention the fact that over the course of our six-year relationship, he neglected to inform me that he had a three-year-old daughter during the time frame that I assumed we were "on again." That was the final deal breaker.

Reading Trey's message that he sent via my inbox, word by word, line by line, in efforts to connect with him on a deeper level, I was amazed at how much we had in common.

"Hello, it's been a long, long time. I'm happy to see you're living someplace warm, especially today, its 7 degrees here. I would like to read some of your writings being that I write as well. I write monthly articles for a men's magazine; I am in the process of writing a book as well, and I do a lot of public speaking events. I am a novice on the whole publishing thing, but I think it's coming along pretty well."

"I am doing well, but it is not exactly warm here in sunny Florida this week. The high today will only be 52 and low will be 27; either way...it's too cold! Who knew that over the years we had so much in common, same resume so to speak. What's your book about?"

"My story is a good one. Its universal in its appeal I think. Its all about how I started my life, shot on three separate occasions, kidnapped, fed indictments, being locked away in the walls of the state correctional institution, then making some life changes, going back to school, building a real estate company, living a jet-set life, dinning with Billionaire's, and walking the Great Wall of China in Beijing a couple of years ago. Its about perseverance, over coming adversity, God's role in our destiny. Its a story about my life—the thing I know best of all, and how my pursuit of success and faith in God holds me down even when I'm not exactly doing what's right. The book is a work progress, although I need to dedicate more time to it."

"Writing a book can be strenuous, but rewarding as well. It is also therapeutic in so many ways. From the looks of it, you have a dynamic story that needs to be told and you never know how powerful your testimony could be to others who are facing adversity in their own lives. I think I will be stopping in Columbus during my book tour this year. I'd love for you to come out."

"Thanks. I will definitely see you then, but I would love to catch up when you have time. Can I call you around 2:00 p.m. tomorrow to catch up?"

"Sure, you can give me a call and I look forward to catching up with you. I will talk to you then."

"Sounds interesting. I can't wait to hear more. Talk to you tomorrow."

With my heart racing and full of apprehension, I sat at my desk and rehearsed every line that I would deliver, anticipated every question I would ask, those he would ask, and how I would respond. I refused to be over anxious and giddy but I would laugh at any jokes he would tell since men love women that laugh at their jokes, even the corny ones.

The following day appeared to be a long one, as I constantly looked at the clock, impatiently I waited for my last client to arrive so I could complete my final therapy session for the day. That day was December 16th, 2011. The sound of his deep and sultry voice had me in a trance; had I been in his presence at that moment, all morals would have been thrown out of the window because his voice alone could have slid me out of my panties. Trey stands 6'3 and weighs in at 235 pounds. His demeanor whispers sexy while his physical being screams tall, dark and handsome. I could tell by his pictures that he was no longer the skinny kid that used to hang out on the block with my brother. He was a professionally dressed, eloquently spoken, gorgeous, fine ass man and the years had been good to him. Standing only at mere 5'4, over the years I have often envisioned him picking me up effortlessly; kissing me passionately and whisking me off into the sunset.

Not getting too ahead of myself and trying to keep my composure, I took the conversation in stride and hung onto every word as he spoke. I was intensely intrigued by him. Aside from the fact that initially I wanted to fuck him, after conversing for hours, I wanted to know him on a personal level and never could I have imagined that this one phone call would be the beginning of many. With my heart still racing and his voice still in my head as I hung up the phone, I stretched out on my bed with a sinister grin on my face. Since distance would be the culprit in this particular situation being that I currently reside in the South and he was in the Midwest, I knew that anything beyond casual conversations was something that was far fetched and could probably never happen. Maybe that's what made the forbidden all the more exciting.

I began to replay our conversation in my head and although we discussed nothing sexual, his voice made my entire body tingle and my pussy wet. I allowed my hands to wander, initially teasing my nipples through my blouse, making them hard; then moving downward towards my tummy. As his succulent voice echoed in my mind, I let my fingers discover my blouse, pulled it up slowly, all the while imagining it was his hands performing the actions. I felt a moan come across my lips and bellowed, "Trey" as I slipped my hand into my panties and inserted my finger into my wet lips. I was amazed at how one conversation with this man, the mere sound of his voice, could have me so aroused.

I closed my eyes and pictured him lying between my legs with a slight smirk on his face, knowing that he was about to please me. I ran my finger over my swollen clitoris and began to make light circles around it, making sure to tease my opening with my index finger. I moaned again, hearing his smooth voice subliminally telling me he wanted to hear me cum. I quickened the pace with my fingers, changing between rubbing my clitoris and slipping my middle finger into my pussy and squeezing against it. My breathing got heavier and my moans were more consistent, almost with each breath. I felt the familiar stirring deep within my body as I started to lose myself in his voice. I pulled my hand from my pussy and climbed out of bed, headed to my closet to get my pink box which contained my favorite vibrator. Getting comfortable on my queen-sized bed, I removed my panties and spread my legs as I laid my head back onto the down pillows that were positioned strategically so that I could love my titties with my tongue. As I inserted my vibrator inside my wet pussy, I squirmed on the bed, and wildly humped it, all the while, wishing that it was him.

Our conversations became a part of my daily routine, we would converse daily for hours discussing all things imaginable from business to politics, and of course, relationships. We were quickly developing a wonderful friendship. All of my days were filled with anticipation wondering when the phone would ring. Being able to discuss my strengths, fears, hopes and aspirations with a man whose primary goal was not to get in between my legs was something I had longed for and it was refreshing as well. Our friendship then took a pleasantly expected turn on Valentine's Day.

"Good Morning."

"Good Morning," I whispered as I was startled by

the ringer from my cell phone ringing at one o'clock in the morning.

"Happy Valentine's Day."

"Happy Valentine's Day to you as well Trey."

"How would you feel if I told you that I booked a flight into Tampa International?"

"How would I feel? I would feel elated, excited and overjoyed!" I yelled hysterically as he laughed on the other end of the phone.

"Well, I will be there in seven hours. I will have a car service pick you up and bring you to the resort."

"Absolutely not! I will be there to pick you up." As grateful as I was for the gesture, I did not want to wait any longer than necessary to lay my eyes on this man.

"You're wonderful, my plane lands at 7:52 a.m."

***

The ride to the airport, which normally takes approximately thirty minutes seemed to be longer. As I approached the airport, nervousness began to set in. Still, I eagerly awaited to receive the text that his plane had landed safely. The adjustment of my black lace panties, last minute make up and hairdo touch up, caused a slight delay in me getting to baggage claim; however, I would soon discover that the slight delay was worth it for him and for me as well. As I gazed down Terminal A, there was Trey and after months of conversation, he remembered that I loved seeing a man in pink and there he was, in a pink button down shirt, starched to perfection; just like him. Waving in a desperate attempt to get his attention, his smile lit up the airport and the masculine scent of his cologne was one that I would never forget.

Words could not even begin to explain how it felt to be in his presence. Trey grabbed my waist, pulled me close and kissed me in a way that I had not been kissed in years. At that moment, I already knew that before the day had even got started, I did not want that moment, that day, to end.

"It's been over twenty years, I'm so happy to see you."

"I'm happy to see you too Trey," I replied trying to discretely hide the tears that were forming behind my Chanel sunglasses.

"Let me grab my luggage and we can leave."

Holding each other close as we patiently waited for his luggage to come across the conveyor belt, I could barely wait until we were alone in our private space. I wanted him now, and for just a moment, I was certain that he was about to become my fantasy turned reality. The same lust and desire that was present in my eyes mirrored the same in his. I wanted to take off my clothes immediately on the spot, uninhibited because I felt as if I had suppressed my sexuality for years up until this new profoundness of him.

After retrieving his luggage, we made our way to the parking garage and again, kissed passionately once inside the vehicle whispering to each other how happy we were at the moment to merely be in each other's presence. As we made our way to our destination, Trey wanted to stop for breakfast at a well-renowned bistro not far from Fletcher Avenue. Upon our arrival at the bistro, we were greeted by a young lady with an accent who welcomed and guided us into a private dining area that he had arranged for us prior to getting there. The room was beautifully decorated with white silk draping the walls, candles lit in lovely brass candelabras, and a place setting for two sat perfectly on the table with tulips adorned in a fine crystal vase. We enjoyed the sound of Luther Vandross gently playing courtesy of the pianist as we indulged in a full course breakfast and my favorite Mango Lime Mimosa's.

"Let's toast," Trey stated as he looked into my eyes.

"Of course, let's. What shall we toast to?" I replied.

"Let's toast to the future."

"To the future." We spoke in unison while the sound of our crystal glasses echoed in the atmosphere as we tapped our glasses together.

As I drank my Mimosa, I felt the warmth of his hand upon my thigh and my body began to respond to his touch as chills overcame my entire body. Motioning the musician to leave and allow us privacy and directing the waitress to remove our dinnerware, he lifted me up on the table and began to run his hands over my body stroking and kissing me gently, while occasionally rolling my nipples between his fingers, pulling them hard, painful at times, yet filled with much desire. My breast were responsive to his touch and like myself, they enjoyed every minute of every touch.

Maneuvering his hand from my breast down to my legs, he spread them open and carefully inserted one finger inside my pussy. He could tell by the scent and the stickiness of my juices that I desperately needed him. Unable to resist the aroma of my sweetness, he buried his head in my pussy and began to work my clitoris until I moaned uncontrollably. Pulling my body down onto his tongue, he began to lick me collectively with both soft and hard strokes, with my juices dripping down his chin and onto his pink shirt.

Knowing that my body was preparing to come, he pulled up his head, stood over me and began to fuck my mouth. I cupped his balls, squeezed and kneaded them, and basked in the enjoyment of his moaning because I knew that I had found his spot. Licking the sides of his penis, he began to get harder and began to thrust faster into my mouth until his body became very relaxed after releasing himself into my mouth with me enjoying every drop.

Trey and I spent the rest of the afternoon sight seeing, shopping, walking the lake and feeding the ducks. Our escapade at the bistro allowed us to temporary suspend our sexual tension that had built up over the last few months, however; still I longed to feel him inside of me and was excited to see what else was in store for the rest of our day.

After a long afternoon, we decided to finally make our way to the resort. The sound of rain that hammered against the window as we were checking in, was a clear indicator that we would not be leaving the grounds for dinner. Making our way to the elevator that led us to an immaculate suite, Trey opened the door and the plush bed was quite welcoming. He sat on the edge of the bed and I sat next to him. With our hands embraced, gazing into each other's eyes, we shared something different--intimacy. Never at a lost for words, the silence served as words unspoken and spoke volumes for us. Soon we embraced, took a shower together and engaged in a much needed nap. With his arms wrapped around me and my head buried in his chest, I felt a sense of comfort that was unfamiliar. I had developed a form of trust with this man that was so profound; and over the months he had became my friend, my lover, and my protector. I knew that anything my heart desired and every fantasy that I wanted fulfilled, he would graciously oblige.

Laying in his arms, I recalled a conversation that we had a few months earlier about the initiation of sex. I have always been reserved sexually, but I knew that I had to make a move to let him know that not only did I need him at that very moment, but I wanted him as well. Placing my petite frame on top of his body, I proceeded to kiss his neck in an attempt to wake him up. Making my way from his neck to his chest, ultimately in between his thighs, and teasingly licking him until he became erect. Teasing his dick with my tongue, he grabbed my head, slowly kissed me and took both of my titties into his mouth. Somehow he had managed to gain control over what was supposed to be my initiation. Although it had been months since I have been sexual with anyone, considering Durrell and I had been broken up for months, I did not want to rush the moment. Also, despite the hardness of his dick, I did not succumb to his desire and made my way back up and began to kiss him; willingly, he reciprocated.

With every kiss, each caress, and the sound of each pleasurable moment, I was getting more excited. My body was screaming for him and after twenty something years of desiring this man, I would get to experience the unthinkable. Turning me over on my stomach, he admired my body and slowly kissed me down my spine before entering me from the back.

"How does it feel?" He whispered in my ear.

"You feel so good daddy! I have been waiting for this moment forever."

"Well, you got me now baby."

"I never want this to end Trey, I never want us to end."

Longing to see in his face, the same sincerity I had heard in his voice, I asked if I could ride him. Slowly I positioned myself on him until all eight inches were inside of me. Skillfully I rode him as he took both of my titties into his mouth, tongued my areola in perfect circles and flicked the nipples with his tongue. Nevertheless, I was impressed with the fact that he had been listening during our conversations as it relates to what my turn-ons and offs were. With the pounding thrusts of him inside of me, my swollen walls welcomed him and we were unable to control ourselves as our bodies rhythmically collided until we came. This Valentine's Day was one that would be remembered forever.

***

It's been a little over a month since Trey and I have seen each other. Still consistent with our telephone calls daily, the days appeared to be longer and I began to miss him more with each passing day. Our connection became like food in order to survive, and we became an addiction to each other and decided that we would see each other on a monthly basis. As each day passed and as the days drew near, I began counting down the hours and minutes until I would see him at Terminal A once again. Wanting to be in total control of our next encounter, I had developed the perfect plan for his next visit, but a plan such as this one would do one or two things; make or break our relationship.

"Hello, this is Chastity with Eros USA, how can I help you?"

"Good Afternoon Chasity, my name is...(pausing) Constance. I'd like to obtain your services for one night."

"No problem Constance, tell me a little bit about what you are seeking and we will develop a package tailored to your needs."

"Sounds great," I replied.

For years, I often fantasized about having a threesome. This has been something that we had discussed and I knew I could trust him with that forbidden desire of mine. He would be in for a complete surprise when he came to visit this month. Five weeks had passed and I was elated about spending the next few days with Trey. Since he put forth so much effort in assuring I was pleased the last time he was in town, it was my duty, as his woman, to return the favor. He flew into Tampa International with a driver this time that I had hired, awaiting to transport him to an undisclosed location. I wanted to add a little mystery to his day, and I needed to buy additional time to build up the nerves to go through with the encounter I had planned for the evening. Soon, he arrived at the Harbor Safety Spa and Resort where I welcomed him into our suite dressed in a long, black silk night gown, with lavender vanilla candles burning, rose petals on the bed, and hundreds of chocolate kisses; he was in awe.

"The suite is beautiful and you are even more beautiful," he said a deep, gentle voice.

"Thank you baby and you look quite handsome yourself. Why don't you take a shower so that we can relax awhile before dinner arrives, I ordered room service," I whispered to him while looking into his eyes.

"Babe...you're the greatest."

As he showered, I wrapped his gift and placed it on the center of the bed. I had purchased him a Hugh Hefner type bathrobe imported direct from Italy and a box of Cuban cigars. Nervously, I drank another shot of Patron; I was probably on my third when the sound of the water ceased, signaling that his shower was complete. Admiring this man as he walked into the room, all I could think about was how utterly sexy he was. This man makes me feel things that I have never felt, he makes my body feel things its never experienced, he feeds my mind and my soul after years of starvation; could I share him with another woman? Or would this be a recipe for disaster?

"Honey, I bought you something."

"You bought me a gift? You are too much babe." I love

when he calls me, "babe." It's one of our many terms of endearments for each other. Anxiously, he unwrapped his gift, put on his bathrobe and like the Nubian king that he is, enjoyed a cigar and then came the knock on the door.

"Honey, could you get the door while I run to the bathroom?"

"Anything for you babe, who is it?'

"Room Service." I hated lying to him, but knowing the circumstances, I was sure that I would be forgiven for this minor discretion.

As he opened the door, there was Chastity, looking exactly like her picture on the Eros website, holding a silver-plated tray in her hand.

"Honey, she is gonna be fucking you tonight and I am going to be making love to you tonight. Enjoy the night honey because tonight is all about you," I said as I stood in the bathroom doorway seductively.

Trey instructed Chastity to sit on the table in front of him, pulled my gown off, started to suck my titties and we kissed each other as I got off the table. She was getting pleasure out of watching two lovers share a moment of intimacy before her role began, this was evident by her sliding her right hand in her jeans and beginning to whimper as she masturbated. Dressed in a black and silver blouse, black lace bra, dark blue denim jeans and Christian Louboutins, she was beautiful, so beautiful even that had I been a lesbian, I would be attracted to her myself. She winked at me and that was my signal that it was time. I commanded Trey to lay in the bed and relax. Making her way to his face, Chastity must have forgotten the rules that I had set forth when I hired her. Under no circumstances was she to kiss him. Kissing was too intimate and that was reserved for us two.

Signaling her to move downward towards his dick so that he could get excited. She took his manhood into her mouth as I kissed my man. He was feeling tremendous pleasure, it was difficult to determine whether the moans stemmed from her giving him oral pleasure or the fact that I had actually gone through with inviting another woman into our bed. I began to feel his hand on my pussy and I began to hump his manly hand as his fingered me.

"Damn, baby. Your pussy is so wet. I would love to see her eat your pussy. Will you let her eat your pussy?"

"Yes baby, I can do that for you."

"So, he wants you and me to give him a show, huh?" Chasity giggled as if she didn't mind.

"Yes, and what my man wants, my man gets so eat my pussy," I sternly ordered.

He proceeded to stroke his hardness as Chasity began to kiss my Cafe' Au Lait body and tenderly sucked my titties before making her way in between my legs, teasing my thighs and eventually my pussy. My legs began to shiver from the pleasure that she was delivering and admittedly, she was good at her job, very good. Quickly I realized why Trey was moaning so damn much. She finally took the top off of the silver platter that unrevealed every lubricant, toy, delicacy and leather whip imaginable, and squeezed a tube of cherry-flavored warming lube on my clitoris and retrieved a strap on and inserted the life-like device inside of me.

"Baby, you look so sexy. Damn my dick is rock hard! Permission to fuck her babe?"

"Permission to fuck her honey," I respond breathlessly.

He stood up, put on a Magnum and straddled Chastity from the back, inserted his long, chocolate rod inside her pink pussy and began thrusting her long and hard. The melody of three people moaning was turning me on tremendously, I was getting even more aroused and observing the look on Chastity's face, she was enjoying him as well. The harder he pounded her, the harder she pounded me. Looking into my eyes he stated, "Baby, I want to make love to you."

Politely I asked Chasity if she would mind if he and I enjoyed each other sexually without her assistance; of course she didn't mind. He quickly moved on top of me and while kissing, I whispered, "I'm all yours." He began to run his hands all over my body feeling me up, picked me up, carried me upstairs to the second bedroom and dropped me on the bed.

"Shit, I have been craving for this pussy for a month," he said as I spread my legs and waited for him to penetrate me, he slowly rubbed my pussy and started to circle his tongue on my waxed mound.

"Trey, honey, please don't stop. You feel so good."

"I won't stop. My job is to please my woman. You taste so good."

Pushing his head towards my pussy so he can taste me a little while longer, I slowly got up, pulled him close and kissed him. Turning around, I made him lie down on the bed, sat on top of him, took his dick into my mouth, in pure sixty-nine fashion as he licked my pussy while I caressed his dick with my mouth. I deep-throated him as if I had not had a meal in days. Unable to take it any longer, I climbed on top of him and guided him inside of me, while my wet, stickiness swallowed him and his manhood disappeared.

"Oh baby your dick feels incredible." My titties were bouncing out of control and Trey had an indescribable hunger in his eyes, he held my hips and as we made love, our bodies collided together recklessly.

"Trey, I'm coming. I'm coming now honey!"

"Cum for daddy baby, cum." He shot his warm load inside of me and at that moment, I had an instant epiphany. Where was Chastity? I still feel kind of bad for abandoning her but she was compensated well and she earned every penny.

"Long distance relationships require a lot of hard work, trust, communication and understanding. Then again, all relationships require hard work and dedication in order to survive. Some say that they are impossible to maintain, but I beg to differ. With two willing adults working towards a common goal together, long distance relationships can very well work. What we have works only because we put in the work to make it work."

Missing Trey terribly, I was eager that the weekend was approaching. This upcoming weekend was his birthday and we have been planning it for a few months now. Not knowing how I could possibly top a threesome as a gift, we decided to merely spend his birthday in a more serene and personable way; just the two of us enjoying each other at my timeshare in Orlando. The time we spent together was beautiful. Never diminishing the times we have spent together before, but as time surpassed, the type of relationship that we had developed was different. For the first time in years, I felt free; as if I did not have to put on a facade' to be accepted by another human being. This man accepted me for the woman that I was without reservation or judgment and I was falling for him and falling for him hard. Being at the timeshare brought back memories of our first encounter, it was raining and it was expected to rain the entire four days that he would be in town.

Our first night was spent talking and reminiscing over dinner because the days prior to his arrival had been hectic for the both of us, and intercourse was that farthest thing from our minds. This was another pleasant change, the fact that we didn't have to be sexual to display intimacy or express our feelings towards each other. We both knew how the other felt and being physical just made the deal more sweet. This night, we merely fell asleep in each other's arms.

***

"Wake up honey, Happy Birthday. Let's get the day started!" I gently said while towering over him with a platter of all the breakfast foods that he adored and a Red Velvet cupcake. I could tell by the look in his eyes that he was so appreciative of the gesture.

"Thank you babe. This is wonderful. What did I do to deserve all that you do for me?"

"You are simply you," I replied.

He shared his breakfast with me, afterwards we playfully engaged in a pillow fight, laughing hysterically, took a shower, got dressed and made our way to the pool to enjoy the lagoon area before the rain started back up. The water was slightly cold so we made our way over to the Jacuzzi. As he began to massage my feet, I began to experience chills down my spine. Every woman loves a foot massage and a man who will rub his woman's feet is a keeper! Always ladylike and never wanting to make a scene, I wanted to be with him right there on the spot. Maneuvering my body in front of his, I began to kiss his neck and whispered in his ear, "I want you." I could tell by the bulge in his swimming trunks that he wanted me as well. Soon, bystanders became company and we were not alone any longer. A few couples from Sweden joined us and we conversed about the culture in their country. Leaning towards my man, I whispered, "Which one of those chicks would you like to fuck?" And to my surprised he replied, "The only woman that I want tonight is you."

Enjoying couple time briefly, the fellas enjoyed beer and cigars and the women sat next to their men listening to them discuss business. I love hearing Trey discuss business, it's one of the many reasons why I am so smitten by him. He was driven by his work and he knew his shit. Hell, I felt as if my man was the most educated man present and I felt proud to be the woman on his arm and it turned me on; I desired him. I suppose the other couples had that same thing as I had in mind, because after a few beers, they were engaged in the ultimate ménage a trois.

They were all fucking each other and after awhile, it was difficult to decipher who were initially coupled up. Since they were consumed with their own entertainment, they were not focused on us. Trey slid my bikini bottoms off and allowed the gravity from the water to lift me onto his penis effortlessly. As the warm waves embraced our bodies, his throbbing muscle massaged my pussy with long, gentle strokes while we French kissed deeply to mask the screams from me coming.

The sight of everyone in the hot tub was one of beauty, and even though my man was not intrigued by the ménage a trois, I was, and I took the liberty to invite Trey and myself into their private affair. By the end of the unexpected rendezvous, we had made a few new friends, business contacts, and engaged in yet another remarkable experience. Afterwards we grabbed our towels graciously and headed back up to our suite to get dressed and prepare for a night out on the town.

Later that evening we attended a Chicago gangster-themed dinner theatre where the cast sang a special tribute to him in honor of his birthday. Delight surfaced in his eyes when they announced his name during their tribute. I became elated that I could bring a level of happiness to his life that he hadn't experienced in quite some time. After the tribute, our waiter made way to our table offering us to help ourselves to the four course buffet. Earlier in the day, we had eaten a fairly large breakfast; therefore, neither of us were very hungry, still, being the gentleman that he is, Trey fixed me a plate filled with all of my favorites which we both enjoyed together along with a few, well maybe more than a few, Capone Rum Runners.

Sitting across from him enjoying the entertainment, I came to another realization and I could hardly wait until the show was over so we could have some quality time alone. The roaring round of applause indicated that the show was over, but for us, the show was just beginning. I handed him the keys to the car to get us to our destination safely being that I was surely over the legal limit to drive.

Back at the resort, I was relieved to get out of the heels that I was wearing, we were both a tad bit over dressed for the occasion, but we both do things with class and style at all times and tonight was no different.

"I really had a great time. This has been the best birthday I have had in over ten years babe. Thank you so much for making my day special," he said while pulling me closer to him by my waist.

"You're welcome. You are so deserving of it all; next year, I'm thinking Paris. What do you think?"

"I think Paris would be great. With your birthday only a month away, I don't know how I can make your day just as special, but I am definitely thinking."

"Honestly, as long as my birthday is spent with you, that's the greatest gift I could ever ask for," I replied.

Gently placing my hand on the center of his chest I pushed him on the bed and began to undress him, I wanted him to feel as if he was the sexiest man alive every moment we were together and to know that I desired him. Stroking him with my hand and tongue in unison, I licked his perineum while he lay helpless in ecstasy as I had my way with him. I continued to allow him to fuck my mouth because I wanted to taste him, all of him. I wanted that part of him inside of me.

"Trey, I want you to try and make me squirt." I knew that this was something that he enjoyed and I wanted to be submissive to his every need.

"Really? Are you sure?"

"I have never been so sure about anything," seductively I answered.

Cupping my mound, he instructed me to relax and give in to what I was feeling. He inserted three fingers inside of me, massaging my G-Spot, and vigorously rubbed my clitoris with his thumb. I hadn't a clue of what was occurring with my body. The sound of gushing waves terrified me, he sensed that fear and assured me that everything was okay and that he would not hurt me.

"Do you want me to stop baby."

"No!" I belted because although it was an unfamiliar sensation, it felt fantastic.

"You're almost there baby, let it go baby."

"Trey, I feel like I'm going to pee on you."

"It's not pee, I promise, let it all go baby, cum for daddy."

"Baby. Hmmm. Baby. It's coming! Fuck, it's coming."

Unable to restrain myself any longer, I squirted all over his face and all over the bed. The small amount of energy that I had left had been ripped from my body at that very moment. My body felt as if it had just received an injection of Novocain. The experience was absolutely amazing. Approximately ten minutes later, somehow I found the strength to get up and bathe. He had drawn the two of us a warm bubble bath and I stepped down into the garden tub and sat between his legs. While he bathed my body, I returned the favor as if he was a fine piece of china that I did not want to get broken. The same way that he wanted to protect me, I wanted to protect him. He asked me something that night, he wanted to know why I was staring at him the way that I stared at him, I told him that it was for no reason, but the truth of the matter was, I was falling in love with him.

"One can't help who they fall in love with; love is more than emotion, it's meeting the legitimate needs of one another, this can be a difficult task. When evaluating whether you love someone or not, question whether it's love or limerence."

Airport bound, we rode in silence listening to the new Marsha Ambrosius CD. It seemed like every song that played in some sort of way delivered a unique message. Reaching over to the passenger's side while placing my hand on top of his, I sang the lyrics to Far Away. This was a bittersweet occasion, another goodbye, yet a day closer to the next thirty days that we'd be together again. As we were arriving at the airport, I received a text from the airline stating that his flight was delayed which afforded us more time to spend together. We decided to go to Friday's for appetizers and drinks. As we enjoyed the smooth jazz of Eric Darius, I heard a soft voice in my left ear. "Well hello there."

The voice was vaguely familiar; however, I could not envision a face with the voice at that time. Perplexed due to our dinner being interrupted because we were already on borrowed time, I swung around in my chair and there was Chastity standing there, looking more beautiful than she had months before. With still over an hour left before Trey's flight was to depart, we checked into the Westin that was on site and made our way to a suite. I wanted him, he wanted me and we both wanted Chastity.

"This encounter is on the house," she proposed.

Aroused by the girl-on-girl action, Trey did not waste valuable time watching, he immediately dug his chocolate rod inside of me while Chastity licked my nipples and fondled his sac. All of our bodies moving frantically as we enjoyed giving pleasure to one another. He pulled me closer, applied a little Anal Ease on my anus; and suddenly I felt him behind me, inch by inch. Careful not to hurt me, he slowly started to move in and out of my ass while Chastity tasted my juices. They were both in sync with each other with their main desire being pleasing me.

"Baby, your ass feels so good on my dick. I love looking at your ass while I fuck you."

"Fuck me harder baby and make me squirt all over her beautiful face," I yelled.

With him stroking harder and she licking faster, an earth shattering orgasm occurred and I creamed all over them both. Not wanting to leave either party feeling neglected, I gave permission for Chastity to be with my man one last time. Placing the condom on him myself, I whispered, "Have fun."

She was craving him and took in every inch he had to offer. They both moved in unison and she was begging for more.

"I wanna cum, you better fuck me good!" she demanded.

With each stride, my nipples became erect and I could not resist sliding my hands into my panties to get myself off. Within five minutes she came. He removed his dick from her and pleasured himself until he came. Glancing over to the clock, I noticed that his flight would be boarding in twenty minutes. Hurriedly, we got ourselves dressed and made our way to the bullet train so that he could make his flight on time. Tears began to form in my eyes. I attempted to hide them, once again, behind my sunglasses. Trey wiped them from my cheeks and comforted me with a gentle kiss promising that he would return next month. Unable to proceed past security, I watched him get on the train in route to the terminal once again to board a plane; this time to Charlotte for business. As I turned and walked away, making my way to the elevators that led to the parking garage, I received a text.

I miss u already. Thank u for a wonderful time. I can't wait 2 c u again.

A year later, Trey and I still talk every day, engage in monthly escapades, and our relationship gets stronger daily; regardless of the distance that separates us. Never could I have predicted that something that began so innocent would evolve into something so beautiful; and that I would find a man who understands me completely, accepts my flaws while still viewing me as the perfect woman for him. Never could I have imagined ever loving a man again and to the degree in which I love him—without conditions. Neither of us can predict where our relationship will go from here, but what we have in each other is a rare find and we intend to continue building the perfect relationship. It may not be the conventional type boy meets girl relationship that's politically or socially correct; but it's the relationship that is perfect for us indeed!

"Never in a million years did I think I'd find someone so utterly and completely perfect; someone who would make me happier than I ever dreamed I could be. Someone that would touch my life so profoundly and just give me a whole new reason to breathe. But then I found you and realized that everything I anticipated

you to be doesn't even compare to who you are."
-Unknown

A Taste of Georgia

By

Ebonee Monique

"Where are my panties?" I moaned loudly as I crawled naked on all fours around the foreign hotel room, like I was searching for a piece of gold.

I dug my fingers into the plush, khaki-colored carpet, glanced around the room and caught a glimpse of myself in one of the mirrors that was hung over a maple table across the room. My hair, which had been curled to perfection the night before, now looked like someone had decided to substitute my head for a Brillo pad and washed a ton of old dishes. I found some sort of sick comfort in knowing that, even though my head looked like a tattered Pomeranian puppy, my make-up was still in tact. How my hair had taken the beating when I had endured a mind-blowing sweat-fest was beyond me. Shaking myself out of the daydream, I remembered that I was crawling on a hotel floor looking for gold.

I guess you could say I was, in fact, searching for gold; in the form of my gold lamè thong underwear, which had mysteriously decided to grow legs and disappear from the spot I'd thrown them in the night before. Isn't it Murphy's Law, though? Just when you need something, it's never where it needs to be and when you don't need it, it's staring you in your face like "Here I am bitch."

Inch by inch, I dug my knees deeper into the floor as I pushed myself forward, looking high and low as I inspected every part of the hotel room.

"I have to find them." I whined to myself as I took a deep breath and plopped down near the foot of the bed.

Here I was, alone in a hotel room that was exquisitely decorated and fancier than any place I'd ever stayed in, and all I wanted to do was go home, throw on my Snuggie, curl up on the couch with a "Girlfriends" marathon, and replay the night before over and over again in my head. But, before I could do that—I needed my drawls. Badly.

I'd toyed with the idea of just abandoning ship after the first two thorough searches around the room, but when I thought about leaving the hotel room commando, with nothing more than my tight black dress that I'd worn the night before, my entire body blushed from embarrassment. The black dress had hugged my body so tightly that the only type of underwear I could wear were the gold lamè fabric thong panties that I'd picked up at a high-end boutique in downtown Atlanta. I'd listened to some uppity red-head with a tattoo on her shoulder blade, tell me that the gold underwear were, "exactly what I needed" to complete my look. She could've told me that invisible drawls were what I needed and I probably would've purchased them.

I got up from the foot of the bed and went to the massive

window that was directly across the room and pulled the curtains back, exposing a ray of sunshine so bright that it caused me to squint my right eye practically closed. The city of Atlanta had never looked so beautiful to me before. I wasn't sure if everything was blissful because I had just had the night of my dreams, or because I had never been in a penthouse hotel room, overlooking a city I'd lived in for close to ten years. Everything looked so small from where I was, and I wondered if there was a way I could capture the moment and put it in my pocket for safe-keeping. When I looked back on my vanilla life fifty years down the line, I wanted to remember this moment as one of the most delectable sprinkles that had ever touched my tongue.

You see, this wasn't me. At all. Not only did I not "hook-up," but I definitely didn't do it with people like Zeus. I was the boring one. You know, the friend you take with you to a club because she's going to have one sip of the fruitiest drink and be finished drinking for the rest of the night. The friend who was the unofficial, official designated driver because, hell, she never did anything at a nightclub but sit in the same spot all night bobbing her head to the music in an attempt to at least look like she was cool. Yeah. That friend. Don't get me wrong, I was loved by many; but I was also predictable. I had the same lunch (tuna fish sandwich on Mondays, Wednesdays and Fridays and a chicken salad sandwich on Tuesdays and Thursdays), sported the same types of cardigan sweaters (a girl can never have too much of a good thing, right?) and had worn my bone-straight hair parted down the middle since I was sixteen. The only thing about me that had changed from sixteen to now was my body. Even I had been pleasantly surprised at the abundance of hips and ass that sprouted out during my Senior year in high school. Still, my cardigans and frumpy khaki's did a great job of hiding things.

I ran my free hand up and down my smooth stomach and allowed it to roam behind me towards one of my plump ass cheeks. I closed my eyes and imagined the moment when Zeus had come from behind me and placed himself directly on my ass. His touch. His breath. His hands. Him. The mere thought of him wanting me, inhaling me, devouring me and filling me, had me so wet I could feel my own juices traveling down my leg.

"No one's going to believe me." I said as I grinned, snapping out of my dirty thoughts. I stroked my hand against the squeaky clean window and stared down to the people on the street below.

I closed my eyes and tried to remember Zeus as he was when I first laid eyes on his naked body the night before. I wanted to devour every morsel of his dark-chocolate toned body with my tongue until I had to beg for a sip of water. My pussy relentlessly throbbed as I thought about how quickly I was ready to fuck him as soon as we had gotten alone. But, see, this isn't me. At least it wasn't me...until he brought out of me what three boyfriends and one finger fuck in high school couldn't: the freak.

I pulled the white bed sheet, which I was using to drape my body, tighter around me and sighed.

"What did you do?" I asked as I grinned slyly to myself just as the in-room phone began to ring, startling me out of my nasty thought.

I wasn't sure if I should answer it. Hell, I knew no one I knew was calling me. My girls probably thought I was home making my famous homemade banana nut bread. They'd never in a million years think I was actually getting my own nut and with Zeus at that. A part of me placed my hand on the phone and picked up the receiver because I wanted to know who it was; I mean, it might've been Diddy or Mary J. Blige... maybe even Beyonce.

"H...H...Hello?" I stammered, trying my best to sound like I was supposed to answer the phone.

"Is...Is Zeus there?" I heard a girl squeal, followed by some giggles from what I could only imagine was a group of her friends standing around her.

"No, I'm sorry he's not here right now." I said coolly.

"Oh my gosh, ya'll!" The girl said as she tried her best to cover the phone with her hand, to muffle her excitement. "This IS Zeus' room!"

I could hear the entire group of girls yell loudly as they quickly all began giggling. I smiled widely.

I sat on the edge of the bed and crossed my legs as I decided to have a little fun with the girls.

"Zeus who?" I asked knowing damn well we all knew who Zeus was. Unless you had been living, breathing and eating underneath the biggest rock on the planet, you knew who Zeus was. Once a part of one of the biggest hip-hop groups around, Residential X, Zeus was and had always been the stand-out star in the group and had since catapulted himself to be one of the biggest stars in the world. In. The. World.

I could hear the girl taking a deep breath and I could only imagine she was rolling her head and about to give me a piece of her mind for not knowing who Zeus was.

"Are you kidding me, lady? Zeus is only the best rapper around. Zeus, aka Matt Anderson? You're answering his phone and don't know that he's on the covers of Black Enterprise, Essence and Ebony all right now? He just opened up five restaurants in California and is about to close a deal on the New York Jaguars basketball team. He's ONLY sold like...I dunno...millions of records and..."

"I get it, sweetie. Thanks for that information." I said kindly. I had started it; she politely finished it.

"So..so...is...like, Matt...I mean, Zeus, coming back?"

"I'm not sure. But if he does, I'll tell him his biggest fan called. What's your name?"

I could hear her gasp "Ch-Chloe. Chloe Judson. O-M-G! Thank you!" She yelled before the phone call dropped.

Taking a deep breath, I fell back on the bed and squealed as I kicked my legs around excitedly. Never in my life had I been so giddy. I peered around the room at my black dress draped over a leather couch and my heels thrown beside the side of the bed, my drawls were the last thing on my mind. I rolled on my side and giggled.

Me...plain ole vanilla, banana nut bread-making Georgia Atkins had gone and done it. I had fucked Zeus.

***

Now let's get one thing straight. I am not a groupie. Well, not the typical—stand outside in the cold until my tits and ass are frozen, just for the chance to nibble on the penis shaft of a celebrity—kind of groupie.

I mean, yes, if you're going off of the fact that I slept with one of the biggest celebrities in the world as being a groupie then maybe...just maybe...I fit into that category. But it was only by chance that it even happened, and I definitely never sought out nibbling on Zeus's penis.

It all started at work two days before.

"Did you get the email about the all-staff meeting, Georgia?" My co-worker Lana yelled over the thin cubicle wall that separated us. I never understood why she asked me dumb questions like that; I always chalked it up to her just needing something to talk about.

"Yeah. It's in five minutes, right? What do you think they're going to talk about?" I asked back, not really needing or caring for the answer.

"Maybe it's something to do with the merger." Lana said quickly. Before I had a chance to respond, she was popping her head around the cubicle wall and grinning her toothy grin in my direction.

"Yeah, maybe that's it." I replied as I crossed my hands together tightly.

I wouldn't say I disliked my job, but I recognized that it was far more in the job category, rather than being a career; which is fueled in passion. Lots of people always tried to figure out what I did for a living, and when I started to try to explain it to them, I'd end up boring myself and just left it at a generic "accounts payable" description. The truth was, I worked for one of the biggest advertising agencies in Atlanta. While I'd been trying to find a way to break into the creative side of the agency, I was far too mousy and quiet to even be considered for anything beyond what I was doing: making calls to collect payment on past due accounts. For someone with a Business degree from Florida A&M University, you would think I would be doing a little bit more than what I was. I was complacent, and not afraid to admit it. It had taken me two years to get my chair to the right level and comfort at work, what was I going to do at a new job and a new chair?

"Well, whatever it is I hope they let us go early. Are you going to the concert?" Lana asked eagerly as she sat down on my counter and cocked her head to the side.

"What concert?"

"Um...The concert. Zeus and Jay-Z are performing at the

Phillips Arena. I heard that Residential X is supposed to be there and even..." Lana commented excitedly as I cut her off by waving my hands.

"No, I'm not going. I couldn't afford tickets that were good enough to warrant me getting dressed up." I lied. I hadn't even looked at ticket prices, let alone looking for something outside of my eggshell cardigan.

Lana and I headed into conference room for our all-staff meeting and I quietly took a seat in the back row and prayed for the meeting to be over. I was pretty sure they were just going to update us on a 401K change or something. But when I saw the CEO of the agency come in with an extra bounce, I shifted in my seat.

Tom Gallagher was the epitome of a privileged man-child. His salt and pepper hair was cut to perfection, perfect for showcasing his boyish good looks. He had to be at least fifty, but had the body of someone who had obviously taken pristine care of himself. I stared at him as he shuffled his papers at the podium and wondered what his life was like. When he drove off in his dark blue two-seater Lexus, did he stress about menial things like paying his bills on time or even what he was going to eat for dinner? I'd heard rumors that his home was a multi-level mansion that was easily one of the biggest homes in Atlanta, equipped with an elevator, two swimming pools and a movie theater. As I tried to remember if I'd put $10 of gas in my two door Honda Civic, I sighed to myself; for once I'd like to live life from the other end.

Tom cleared his throat and everyone who was chattering, quickly turned their attention towards him. He straightened out his red and blue tie as a smile crept over his face.

"Well, as you all know, we've been trying for years to get the Phillips Arena to sign on as clients. Thanks to the hard work of our creative services team and select members of our accounts payable team, we were able to secure them as of late yesterday!"

A little bit of myself beamed on the inside. I know that I had played a bit of a small part in bringing Phillips Arena around to our agency, and I wondered if I was the select member of the accounts payable team that Tom was speaking of.

My best friend Sandra had worked at the Phillips Arena in the promotions department for close to seven years, and because of our relationship, she was able to subtly drop the idea of working with our agency to her executive team. After months and months of subtly dropping hints, Sandra went in for the kill and finally made some progress. When I got the call three months earlier, that Phillips Arena was requesting a proposal from our agency, I yelped. Then I coolly went into Tom's office and announced the great news. I probably would have felt weird about Tom wrapping his pasty, cold hands around me and hugging me so tightly, if I hadn't realized just how major it was for the arena to even contact us for a proposal.

I grinned widely as I nodded my head in Tom's direction.

"This is a great day for our agency. We should all be proud. Let's give ourselves a round of applause." Tom said as he started the slow clap that movies were made of. As if in sync, everyone fell in line and followed his lead.

Once the applause had died down, Tom continued to speak.

"Georgia...Georgia Atkins, come up here."

Lana nudged me with her elbow and whispered "Oh shit, girl." as I took a deep breath and stood and walked before my colleagues. I knew half the people in the fifty-person office didn't even know my name, let alone that I knew how to speak. I walked up the narrow aisle, past all of the "popular" work folks and giggled inside. Standing next to Tom, I clasped my hands together tightly. It was the only way I knew how to not look nervous.

"Many of you don't know Georgia is one of the main reasons we got the green light to even present to Phillips Arena." Tom said as he nodded proudly. "Georgia has been a dedicated employee, and her recent efforts have gone above and beyond anything that's written in her job description." Tom said as he inched closer to me and pulled out an envelope.

"It seems like a lot of people here don't know Georgia too well." Tom laughed awkwardly. I nervously giggled as well, wondering where he was going with this. If it wasn't obvious enough by the fact that the only person I talked to at work was my cubicle neighbor, I didn't need Tom rubbing it in.

"We were trying to do a little research on you—you know, to show just how thankful we are for dedicated employees— and it seemed like every road we tried came up to be a dead end. But, thanks to Lana and her investigative skills, we came to find out that you're a big fan of Zeus, the rapper, right?"

I wasn't sure why my face felt like it was beet red. I mean, I was allowed to like what I liked, but it was awkward to have my small crush placed on display in front of a room full of people that wouldn't have even blinked if I'd sneezed. Lana had overheard me talking on the phone about Zeus one day to Sandra and ever since, she had been content with using that one piece of personal information to her advantage. Every conversation started off about Zeus. Every IM chat began with a Zeus one-liner. Every phone call ended with "Zeus" instead of "Deuce." If you were a fly on the wall of our conversations, you might have thought I was an obsessed Zeus freak. In reality,

I respected him, hell, I even thought he was handsome; but Lana had made up in her mind that I played with myself at night because of the mention of his name.

"Yes. I'm a fan of his work." I said as I cleared my throat and widened my eyes in Lana's direction. What the hell had Lana told this man? Probably that I lined my walls at home with magazine tear-outs of Zeus.

"Well, we know that Zeus is going to be at the Phillips Arena tomorrow night and we also know that you don't have tickets. On behalf of the agency, we wanted to get you something we know you wouldn't normally treat yourself to." Tom commented as he handed me an envelope that felt too heavy to be just a card and too light to just be a CD.

I took the envelope and smiled like an idiot. I never know how you're supposed to handle public card giving. Do you open it then and squeal madly, even if you're not impressed by the gift? Or go home and open it alone?

Tom must have sensed my confusion on whether or not to open the envelope. "Go ahead and open it! We want to see your reaction." Tom said wide-eyed and excited-like. If I wasn't sure of who I was, I'd think Tom thought he was gifting a meal to a homeless person. I made a mental note to strangle Lana when we returned to cube-land.

I slowly broke the gold-colored seal open from the back of the dark colored envelope and pulled the contents of it out. The first thing my eyes caught were tickets. Inside, I squealed. They couldn't have been Zeus tickets. No way. Upon further inspection I saw that it was not only two tickets, but two sky box passes, two VIP passes, a parking pass and a $500 American Express gift card. That was it, I'd played it cool enough.

"Tom...I don't think I can say thank you enough. This was

all really unnecessary." I said clutching the envelope tightly. Tom reached over and patted me on my shoulder and grinned widely.

"Thank you for all of your hard work, Georgia."

I shuffled back to my seat as Tom continued talking about a few other housekeeping items. I tried to focus on what he was saying, but I couldn't. My mind was racing a million miles a minute. I was going to have to figure out what to wear, how to do my hair and who to invite. It wasn't until I saw everyone stand up and begin filing out of the room that I realized we'd been dismissed from the meeting.

"Are you happy?!" Lana yelped as we headed back to our cubes. I was more in shock than anything. I nodded my head and continued looking at the envelope.

"And you get the rest of today AND tomorrow off? I'm jealous."

"Wait...what?" I asked looking up.

"Weren't you paying attention in there? Tom said we get the rest of the day off today and you get Friday off as well. Earth to Georgia."

Lana and I made small talk as we headed down to our cars.

"Take lots of pictures, Georgia. Like, lots." Lana repeated, like I'd missed it the first time.

I promised Lana to come back with a full report on Monday. I couldn't believe it. Not only did I have the entire rest of the day off but I had an extended weekend and would be enjoying a concert to see my favorite entertainer. As soon as I saw Lana's Volvo pull out of the parking garage, I scrambled to my purse to examine the contents of the envelope again. I ran my fingers over the sky box passes and giggled as I dialed Sandra's number.

"Hey boo." She said in a hurried tone. I could already tell my time with her on the phone was limited so I kept it short.

"So, who's going to Zeus and Jay-Z's concert tomorrow, with VIP and skybox passes?" I asked in an ecstatic tone.

I could hear Sandra shuffling around papers and could imagine her balancing the phone in one hand as she searched for an unnamed object with the other.

"Who? What?" She asked. I could tell I had her attention. "You're lying!"

"I swear!" I laughed. "I just got them for helping to close the account with Phillips Arena and the agency and...well... since you were key in getting everything together, I figured you'd go with me! I have two of everything!"

I almost couldn't contain my excitement long enough to get everything out. Sandra loved Zeus just about as much as I did and I already knew she'd been trying her best to find a way to work her way into the concert. Even working for the arena, it was difficult for a Phillips Arena employee to get into the concert. It was that exclusive and guarded.

"You're lying to me Georgia Atkins. You better be lying." Sandra said, sounding like she was whining. I could pick up on the disappointment in her voice before she said anything.

"Why do you sound like that? You should be excited." I replied slowly as I watched a few more co-workers pull out of the parking garage.

"I would be excited if I could go." Sandra sighed heavily. "I got roped into watching my baby cousin for the weekend while my aunt and uncle go out of town. They've planned this whole trip around being able to have me as a babysitter."

I tossed my head back on the headrest and took a deep breath. I would be lying if I said I wasn't disappointed. Besides Sandra, I had two other girlfriends, but neither of them were interested in Zeus and I knew they would only make my night miserable by complaining about the loud music, crowd and ambiance.

"So what am I supposed to do?" I asked in a child-like manner. Sandra was my partner in crime. Wherever I went, she went. Whatever she did, I did.

"Um, you're going to take your ass to that concert. What do you mean?" She quizzed. I could tell she was about to give me an earful.

"Just because I can't go doesn't mean you're going to pass up the opportunity that both of us have dreamed about. Hell, when else will you have a chance to not only see Jay-Z perform but Zeus too? When I get off tonight we're going to find you something cute to wear and you're going to take your ass to that concert and have the time of your life."

I exhaled and wondered if I was ready to venture out to events by myself. As silly as it sounded, I was so used to having my crutch, Sandra, there with me that the mere thought of having to enter a room by myself gave me gas.

"You hear me?" Sandra yelled, yanking me out of my daydream.

"Yeah, I hear you. I just wish you could come."

"Well, I can't, so we have to deal with the reality at hand." Sandra said quickly.

That's what I loved about Sandra. In a matter of minutes she could take an empty glass and squeeze some juice from an unknown source and make it seem delightful. Her pleasant personality and even more pleasant looks made it so easy to be her side-kick. With her short, Halle Berry-inspired hair-do and cute chinky eyes, Sandra had a way of making people— men and women alike—flock to her without trying. I envied her, but I never let that envy override my love for her. Sandra had a mentality about her that made her desirable to men, but she had enough smarts to never place her emotions before her common sense. I wouldn't say my friend got around, but she definitely had her fair share of fine men and wasn't shy about her "Fuck them and leave them" attitude.

"Call me when you get off." I said, plastering a smile on my face.

I pulled out of the garage and decided to head home and kill the rest of the afternoon the best way I knew how to: doing plain ole vanilla activities.

***

By the time I got to the cute little boutique in downtown Atlanta, that Sandra had told me to meet her at, the sun was setting and I was not in the mood to shop.

"Hey. Traffic was a beast. Sorry I'm late." I sighed, opening my purse and revealing a wrapped loaf of banana nut bread to her.

"I swear you're going to make me fat as hell, girl." Sandra laughed as we embraced.

"You could use some fattening up." I joked as I pinched at her non-existent waist.

The boutique was cute. Not at all pretentious like most of the downtown Atlanta boutiques I'd been in before. Old school hip-hop blared from the speakers while a young, hip looking saleswoman smiled widely at the two of us.

Sandra grabbed my hand and pulled me towards the rack she had been standing at.

"Okay. I have three choices. All of them are hot too. 'Cause, girl, we have to make sure you are on P-O-I-N-T tomorrow. You can't be meeting Jay-Z and Zeus looking a hot..." Sandra said as I cut her off.

"I don't even know if I want to go anymore." I shrugged as I fiddled with one of the dresses on the rack.

Sandra stepped back from me, almost like I had the plague, and looked me up and down for a few seconds before letting out a comical, "Yeah right!" and turning her attention back to the rack of clothes.

"I'm serious, Sandra. You know how I am. I can't just...I don't know...go somewhere by myself. That's you not me. I'm boring Georgia; not fun Sandra. And then, on top of that, you want me to meet Zeus? I don't know..." I trailed off, knowing Sandra wasn't letting this go that easily. She never did.

"You know why people think you're boring? Because you think you're boring. Why do you do that to yourself? You don't need me or anyone else to validate how kick ass of a person you are. You're young, beautiful, single and fun as hell, once you let yourself let loose. It's not by chance that you got this wonderful opportunity and I'll be damned if you don't go and have fun. Okay?"

I would have been a fool to object, so I just nodded my head.

"Now try these on." She said shoving the dresses my way.

I shimmied my way in and out of three of the dresses and was convinced the fact that all of them made me look like throw-up in a blanket had to be confirmation that I didn't need to go; that is, until I tried on dress number four. The one-shoulder Dauxilly dress was sheer on the top, with selectively placed gold and black sequin patches over my breasts and a spandex bottom. To say it fit like a glove would be an understatement.

"That's it! Ring it up now!" Sandra yelled as soon as I stepped out of the dressing room.

I turned and looked at myself a few times, trying to make

sure that it was my rotund ass, flat stomach and perky tits staring back at me. I moved my long hair to the side and felt a surge of confidence that I'd never felt before.

"I made you an appointment at The Glambar Salon on Peters Street. They're going to get you beautified tomorrow at 4:00 p.m. You'll get ready there. They have showers and everything." Sandra said as she rubbed her hands together like a mad woman.

"I'm getting ready at the salon?" I asked as I tossed the bags into my car and looked over at my best friend.

"Yes, they'll take care of you; hair, makeup, nails, pedicure...everything! Bring everything with you!"

"If you say so." I laughed as I hugged her tightly. "Thanks for everything, girl."

We got into our cars and I reached over to look at my cell phone like someone had really called me, and saw the banana nut bread still sitting in my purse.

"Ooh, Sandra, wait! Your bread!" I jogged over to her four-door dark blue Mazda and tapped on the window. I could see my friend laughing to herself at how lame I was.

"What am I going to do with you and this damn banana nut bread?" She chuckled as she took it from me and placed it in the passenger seat. "Now, if I could only get you to put the moves on Zeus like you do some damn bread."

"Hey you never know." I lied, knowing I'd piss my pants if I was ever in the same room alone with him.

"Yeah, right. And unlimited dildos are going to drop from the sky tonight." Sandra giggled shaking her head.

I wasn't offended, but something about the way she was so damn convinced that I couldn't even handle flirting stung my pride.

I shrugged my shoulders and looked at a car zooming by.

"I wish for once you'd let your hair down and just get one good fuck in. I swear it'd clear all of your up-tightness up." Sandra laughed.

I thought about what Sandra said on the entire ride home. I wondered if I was equipped to handle flirting. Or more. That night, I fell asleep listening to some old school R&B, wondering how I could transform fear into confidence.

***

When I walked into the Phillips Arena, I was sure that I had toilet paper stuck to my stilettos by the number of stares I was getting. I wasn't used to that kind of attention. Since I had just gotten my pussy waxed earlier that day, I was feeling every sensation—especially the moistness. I wasn't sure what had prompted me to get my first Brazilian wax that morning, but as I headed into Sweet Samba waxing center, I felt a sense of urgency to tend to all of my areas. I guess you could call it a fucking premonition. Pun intended.

I found my way to the sky box area, got a vodka and cranberry drink and relaxed. Of course, typical Georgia, I'd arrived earlier than anyone else and was the first one in the sky box. I went through my purse and remembered I had the VIP passes and wondered what to do with them.

"Excuse me. What do I do with this pass?" I asked kindly to an usher as I slowly sipped my drink. One vodka and cranberry drink was enough to have me buzzed and here I was drinking it like it was Kool-aid.

"Oh, honey, I think you go down to the first level and go to your immediate right and you should see the VIP section. You might want to hurry." The grey-haired woman said as she checked her watch. "I think they close down the VIP meet and greet in about twenty minutes."

I chugged the last of my drink and hustled my way down to the area I'd been instructed.

"Pass please." The overweight security guard said as I approached the door labeled, "VIP Meet and Greet."

After I flashed my credentials and made my way against the concrete wall, behind the other seven ladies lined up, I looked around. I was the last person in line and, by far, the most over-dressed. The other girls in front of me had on skinny jeans and crop-topped shirts. I looked like I was auditioning for a lead in a music video and they looked like they were auditioning to be the people who steamed the clothes the leads wore in the music videos. Tugging at my dress, I moved slowly as the line crept up a bit.

"Damn." I heard a voice say to my right. I didn't turn to look because, hell, I was sure they weren't talking to me.

"What's your name?" The voice inquired as I felt a hand gently tap my shoulder.

I turned around and smiled. I recognized his chiseled face as being one of Zeus's closest childhood friends, Tarik. He had been in virtually every music video, interview, attended every basketball game courtside and every outing beside Zeus. Anyone who knew Zeus, knew Tarik. He stood about six feet tall and had the most piercing set of eyes I'd ever seen. He was sporting a black t-shirt, a pair of jeans and a black and white pair of Jordans while an army-fatigued hat sat on top of his head.

"I'm...I'm...I'm Georgia." I stammered, trying to pull it together.

Tarik took my hand, shook it and stepped back and took all of me in. I could say I felt weird about his eyes piercing me, but I didn't.

"Damn, Georgia. You're bad as hell." Tarik said biting his bottom lip and looking at me in my eyes. "My name is Tarik. You here with anyone?"

"No. I came by myself."

"Well, damn...where are your seats?"

"In one of the sky boxes." I replied quickly as I shifted my stance and tilted my head.

"That's wassup! Well, hopefully I see you later on tonight. We're supposed to be partying at Club Empire, you know where that is?"

I nodded my head as Tarik walked away.

"Shit." I heard Tarik say again as he checked my rear-end out while I crept closer to the room where the meet and greet was being held.

By the time I got to the door, there were two other girls in front of me, and I heard them begin to grunt and take deep sighs. One of the girls smacked her teeth really loudly before turning back to me and saying, "These motherfuckers better not try me. They don't know what I had to do in order to get these VIP tickets." She said tossing back her 24' inch weave.

"What? Are they closing the line or something?" I asked raising an eyebrow.

"That's what they're trying to say." The other girl, who looked like a mousy librarian, said quietly. I hadn't done anything outlandish to get the VIP passes, like 'weave girl,' but I'd waited in line, gotten my pussy waxed, my makeup, hair, nails and feet done for the five minutes I was promised to take a VIP picture with Zeus and Jay-Z.

"Sorry ladies. The Meet and Greet is closed. The artists have got to get ready for their sets, so we've got some autographed photos for you, but nobody else will be permitted beyond this point." Another two-ton security guard said as he nonchalantly passed out the black and white glossy photos of Jay-Z and Zeus.

"What the fuck do you mean?" Weave girl screamed, as she tried to make a dash to the door knob. I had to admit, I didn't blame her for acting out but I damn sure wasn't about to lose my newly found "cool" in public. I took a deep breath and headed back to the door I'd come in. I should've known something like this was going to happen. How could I have expected anything differently? I had every mind to think about heading back to my car and driving home. I still had enough time to curl up on the couch and catch a re-run of 'The Game' on BET.

"Where you going, Georgia?" I heard the familiar voice ask, just as I placed my hand on the door to leave the VIP section.

Turning around, I saw Tarik looking baffled. "You're leaving already?"

"They closed the meet and greet section. So, yeah."

Tarik tossed his head back, smiled and grabbed my arm. "Come on, girl. You're with me."

I passed by the two girls that had been standing in front of me and dropped my head. Part of me felt like shit for not grabbing them and taking them with me; part of me didn't want to mess the opportunity up for myself. Tarik approached the door, gave the security guy dap and we pushed through. I felt like royalty. Like I'd been granted entrance into a secret society all because I'd worn the magical gown, crown and shoes to the ball.

The room looked like a typical dressing room. I looked around the beige-colored walls and paid attention to all of the hustle and bustle going on around the room. People were moving with intensity, while others lit up joints and smoked them casually.

Then I saw Zeus. All six foot five of him. I know, for a fact, that I came in those gold lamè thong panties right then and there. I was pretty sure Tarik was saying something to Zeus about me, because I saw his mouth moving, but I didn't hear anything. All I saw was this beautiful, dark chocolate-skinned man with the prettiest set of white teeth I'd ever seen. I wanted him right then and there. I'd never in my life been so attracted to someone so instantaneously. My pussy throbbed something ridiculous as I saw Zeus approach me.

"Hey. Nice to meet you, Georgia." He said kindly. I surveyed his face for a few seconds before I snapped out of it.

"Hi...Hey." I said smiling so widely that my cheeks began to hurt. "It's a pleasure to meet you."

Zeus leaned down and hugged me tightly, like we'd known each other for years. I inhaled his delicious scent of Egyptian Musk and exhaled slowly. I wanted to savor the moment.

"Sorry about them closing the meet and greet." Zeus said as he inched closer to me.

"No. It's okay. I'm just glad to even be here."

"Well, you missed Jay. They got him out of here as soon as they closed the doors." Zeus said as he motioned for me to follow him to a seating area. Tarik followed us, acting like he was playing on his Blackberry.

I smiled as I followed Zeus' suit and sat down in the chair beside his.

"Yo, Tarik! Will you go make sure they got all the wardrobe shit together? I can't have them putting me in any wack clothes this time. We're in Atlanta." Zeus said with a raised eyebrow.

Tarik hesitated and then sauntered out. There were still a few people buzzing around the room, doing everything and nothing in particular.

"So where are your girls? I know you didn't come by yourself." Zeus said staring at my legs as I crossed them.

"Actually I came alone." I was feeling my buzz kicking in and the confidence was beginning to ooze from my pores.

"Word?" Zeus said with a grin on his face. "That's pretty dope."

I felt a certain comfort with him; maybe it was the liquor or maybe it was my slippery wet pussy. I leaned into him and chuckled.

"Why do you say that?" I asked biting my bottom lip as I imagined how his plump lips would taste against mine. They were the right size for great pussy eating but, as my mind took me elsewhere, I wondered what they would feel like pressed against my lips.

Zeus finished off the bottle of water in his hand and licked his lips of the remnants. It's like he knew what I was honing in on. I wanted to suck those lips with such ferocity that he had to ask for permission to have them back.

"It's not a lot of women that would go anywhere by themselves. That's just real dope."

I smiled before replying.

"I wouldn't miss out on this opportunity just because I didn't have anyone to go with. Then I never would've met you."

I heard myself say the words but I wasn't sure where they were coming from. They were genuine...but they weren't vanilla Georgia.

Zeus examined my face for a while and licked his lips. It was all the confirmation I needed that he was attracted to me.

"You know, I haven't been back to Atlanta to perform in a few years. I don't know how that's happened though. I love Georgia. Georgia's always been good to me."

In my mind, I said "Georgia loves you back and I will fuck

you something good" but I kept it cool, calm and collected and maintained my idiot-grin.

Tarik came back in the room with a look of urgency.

"Aye, they need you for something in the dressing room." Tarik said quickly, with his Blackberry pinned to his face.

Zeus nodded his head and stood up, prompting me to do the same. He then leaned into me and gave me another hug.

"It was really great meeting you" He whispered into my ear.

"You too." I said pulling away.

I was sure that was going to be the end of our chance encounter as I watched four people, including Tarik, flank him as he exited the room; but when he held up a finger to all of them and came back to me, I stopped breathing.

"You need to have my number. Maybe we can hang out or something later."

I wasn't dumb; I knew "hang out" was code for doing the horizontal tango. As I punched his number in my phone, I wondered if I even had the nerve to go through with it.

"Call me now so I can lock you in." He said quickly. I did as I was told and watched those beautiful white teeth appear when my number blinked on his phone.

"Got it." He said with a wink.

I watched his powerful, seductive, delicious ass stroll out of the room and I took a deep breath. I probably would never hear from or see Zeus again but as I looked at my phone and saw his number staring back at me, my non-vanilla thoughts began racing.

Suddenly, my walk became an easy one—filled with sass and confidence—and I didn't have to wonder if I had tissue pinned to my shoe. I was the bad bitch they were staring at and my vodka-induced confidence was going to lead me to places, heights and orgasms I'd never seen or felt before.

***

My lips tingled as I stared at myself in my rear-view mirror just as my phone buzzed.

It was Zeus.

We had already been texting about "hanging out" since the concert let out. When my phone buzzed shortly after the concert ended, I had to contemplate either never seeing him again or, for once, stepping out of the vanilla ice cream carton and into something a little more flavorful and daring.

"Hey, beautiful." He said softly.

"Hey yourself." I replied closing my eyes, "What room are you in?"

"222. Are you coming?"

"On the way up now." I said almost too quickly.

I checked my hair and makeup and popped a peppermint before making the stroll to the entrance. I watched myself in the mirrors that lined the elevator and I smiled. My heart was racing as I took the steps towards the direction of room 222. Just as I went to knock on the door, I felt my phone ring. Looking down at it, I saw it was Sandra. I had to make a quick decision to send my best friend to voicemail. What I was doing was not for her or because of her words to me the night before; it was strictly because my pussy was being pulled in by Zeus. The moment he had looked in my direction and licked his lips, I'd had visions of riding him until I left a puddle on his stomach.

"Hey. Come in." Zeus said with a grin after I knocked on the door. He was still dressed in a black t-shirt, a pair of jeans, a black hat and black and white Converse Chuck Taylor's. Had I been okay with being arrested for rape, I would have fucked him right there, door open and everything.

"Have a shot at the bar with me." He said as he motioned with his head. I had been drinking enough and I knew it, so I declined.

"At least take a shot with me." He said playfully as he gripped my waist and pulled me towards the fancy bar. Before I knew it we were downing two shots of Silver Patron and were talking life stories.

"How did you get Zeus from Matt? That's your real name, right?" I slurred from the left side of the bed.

"I've always been into Greek mythology. I don't know why. Zeus just seemed to be the powerful god that was always listened to."

"He was also married to his sister that he cheated on with mortals. You're married, right?"

I saw Zeus' cheeks lift while he slowly raised his eyes to mine. I'd said either the words that were going to get my ass kicked out or fucked righteously. I was hoping for the latter.

"I am married." He replied "How do you know so much about Zeus the god?"

"I studied Greek gods in high school and fell in love with them. Zeus was the most intriguing. Even with all of his imperfections." I said swallowing the lump in my throat.

I laid back on the pillow and took a deep breath.

Without as much of a word, Zeus disappeared to the bathroom and soon I heard the shower come on. I assumed he was giving me the opportunity to make the decision as to whether or not I wanted to leave.

When he returned to the room, with nothing more than a towel wrapped around his waist, my eyes traced up and down his body like he was a piece of chocolate, waiting to be devoured slowly in my mouth.

"Do you mind if I take a shower?" I heard myself ask as I

stood up and made my way towards him.

Zeus smiled, as relief spread on his face.

"Be my guest."

I took a thorough shower, making sure to allow the soap and warm water to hit every spot of my body. I ran my hands up and down my soft skin, stopping right at my bare pussy. I allowed my fingers to play with my clitoris. I tossed my head back and imagined my fingers replaced with Zeus's tongue. I was dripping wet and was ready for whatever was about to go down.

I returned to the room with a towel covering my torso and chest, to find Zeus laying in bed with one hand behind his head and the other used to flip through the channels with the remote with his towel still wrapped around his waist. He looked like a dream. An absolute fucking dream. I went to the other side of the bed and sat down quietly. Before I could even begin to think about what I was doing, I had removed my towel and scurried directly under the nook of Zeus's armpit. I felt at home.

In seconds, Zeus turned the television off and reached over on the nightstand and hit a button on his iPad starting, what I could only imagine was, a "fuck me" play-list of smooth sounds.

"You're so beautiful." He cooed as he ran his tongue from my ear to my neck. I had never felt a feeling so tantalizing and it was only his tongue. I wondered what the bulge that was peeking out from beneath his towel would do to my body. I couldn't speak. My mouth wanted to say, "Just fuck me now." But I bit my lip and breathed in and out slowly.

Zeus pulled away from me and looked in my eyes. The same eyes I'd seen on television, posters and on countless CD covers were staring back at me with an intense desire.

"Do you mind if I kiss you?" He asked sweetly.

"Please." I begged as I pressed my naked body into his.

His mouth devoured mine. I felt his thick tongue playing inside of my mouth and I wanted to melt right there. I cupped his smooth, chocolate face in my hands and pulled him closer. I traced the outside of his lips with my tongue, making sure to get every line and curve his lips were offering me.

"Stop." I heard myself say to him, "Let me kiss you. I want to do the work."

I could see Zeus wasn't used to having a woman be interested in pleasing him with kisses. I wanted to plant them all over him. I let my tongue do the walking and took his light moans as an indicator that he was enjoying it. I nibbled on his bottom lip as I ran my hands up and down his body. I wanted to get to the fucking, but I didn't want to miss a spot either.

"Damn girl." I heard him say as he opened his eyes and locked in on me. I bit down on my lip and allowed my hand to trail his body all the way to the rock hard, chocolate cock that was standing at attention just for me. I had to see it; feeling it wouldn't be enough. I stroked my hand around his dick and gripped it tightly. He had to be at least nine inches of pure, rock-hard manhood. I couldn't stop licking my lips if I wanted to. I wanted to taste it, slurp it and suck it dry. But before I could do anything, Zeus was pushing me on my back. He took both of my breasts in his hands and examined them closely before placing his mouth on one, flicking his tongue around eagerly. He traced his tongue around my entire breast and sucked my nipple until he got them hard as rocks.

After attending to both of my breasts and aggressively pinching my nipples in his hands, to the point of creating an unrecognizable moan from my mouth, he took his tongue and trailed it from my breasts to my stomach. I watched closely as he spread my legs and allowed his tongue to go from my stomach to my pelvis area before placing gentle kisses on my inner thigh. In no time, he was diving face first in my pussy like he hadn't had been fed in days. I felt his tongue playing hide-n-seek and I yelped. I hadn't been ate like that in years, and I could tell his tongue was having the time of its life. I heard him slurping and licking loudly in between his muffles of "This shit is so good." He lifted my legs up, to get a better position, and traced his tongue from the softest place on earth to the brim of my asshole. He delicately flicked his tongue around, causing me to squirm in excitement. My body was having all types of convulsions as it tried to keep it together and not bust all over Zeus' face. He gripped my waist as he continued to allow me to fuck his face. I gripped the back of his neck and pulled his face deeper into me.

I could feel the wetness from my pussy dripping everywhere, and as Zeus stuck one finger inside of me, he gasped at how wet I was too.

"Shit, baby. You're wet as fuck." He moaned as he stuck his head back between my legs and began to lick my clit while fingering the fuck out of my pussy. I hoisted my hips off of the bed, watching as Zeus followed his prize with an eager tongue. I bit my bottom lip and moaned softly.

I felt a painful pleasure as Zeus inserted another finger inside of me. If his finger-fucking and pussy eating was any indication of his straight fucking, I wanted to hurry up and get to the main course. I looked down at Zeus as our eyes locked. He had a mouthful of me...was watching me closely, taking in my every reaction. I tossed my head backwards and arched my back. I was on the brink of letting my juices off in his mouth in a major way. I gripped the back of his head and began humping my pelvis towards his face. I needed to meet the tip of his tongue with the tip of my clit, something serious. I felt the tingle in my spine coming up quickly, letting me know I was approaching the point of no return.

"Oh shit!" I yelled as I gripped his neck tightly and allowed his tongue to hit my sensitive clit just as I came harder than I had ever came in my life.

My legs shook terribly as I tried to regain my composure. Zeus took his tongue and continued kissing around my pussy and inner thigh, but I'd had enough of him pleasing me. I needed to feel his dick in the back of my throat.

"Lay back." I said with attitude. He wasn't going to show me up. I was determined to make his toes curl, his eyes roll and his dick touch my tonsils.

I straddled him and quickly moved my body down so that I was face-to-face with his penis. I gripped it tightly with one hand and placed my other hand on his firm thigh. I just wanted to make him cum, preferably all on me. I kept a firm grip on his dick and quickly placed it inside of my mouth. I heard him sigh heavily as he plopped his head back on the pillow. Then, I went to work. If I didn't know how to do anything else, I knew how to suck some dick. I thought of dick sucking like an art form. It was all in the suction, hand-movement, wetness and intensity. More than anything, though, it was about passion. Men could tell when you're only sucking them off out of obligation versus wanting to devour the head of his dick with everything you had.

I allowed him to go in and out of my mouth, making sure to keep a tight suction around his penis. I pulled my head back and gathered a mouth full of spit and made sure to cover his dick in it. Then I went back to bobbing my head up and down. I jacked his dick off at the same time as I was sucking him and watched as his body twitched heavily. I traced my tongue around the smooth, defined head and made sure to suck delicately around it. I pulled back from his penis again and took in the sight of it. It was so beautiful, so brown, so hard and—for the moment—so mine. I lifted his dick up and went lower, making sure to get his balls in my mouth. I continued jacking his dick off while I played with his sensitive balls with my tongue.

"Shit, Georgia. Shit." Zeus said as he lifted his head up and watched me closely.

I continued pulling my tongue from the top of his ball sack to the back, making sure to allow every area of his balls the pleasure of meeting my tongue. I let go of his dick, letting it hit my forehead, and I could tell that drove him crazy. He gripped his dick and pulled me up by the back of my neck and forced his dick back into my mouth. I loved the fact that he was fucking my face so aggressively. I could feel his hips thrusting towards my face and I made sure to extend my tongue, to allow room for all nine inches of his dick.

"Deep-throat that shit, baby." He said in a soft moan.

I took his dick from his hand and decided to show him just who he was messing with. I took his dick deep into the back of my throat until I felt tears forming in my eyes and I felt myself choking. I gagged once I felt the furthest his dick would go. I pulled his dick out and slapped it against my face a few times before I felt the familiar pulse of a dick ready to blow. I put him back in my mouth and bobbed up and down on him, making sure to keep my lips wrapped around his dick like it was going out of style. Before I knew it, I heard his toes popping and knew it was time.

"I'm cumming." He yelled loudly. I wrapped my lips around his dick and sucked heartily until I felt the warmth of his cum dripping down the back of my throat. I was too busy continuing to suck up the rest of his juices to notice that Zeus was pulling me up towards him. Immediately he wrapped his lips around mine and bit my bottom lip.

"You tasted so delicious, Georgia. Shit I can't wait to fuck you." He said through heavy breaths while he nibbled on my lips. I ran my hands up and down his rock hard body and didn't even have the words to describe how ready my pussy was for him.

Zeus reached into the nightstand beside the bed and pulled out a condom. In record time, he had applied it and had spread my legs to the perfect degree as I laid on my back. I wanted to see his face when he entered my pussy. I knew it was tight, wet and I knew his dick was going to curve to me perfectly. Again, call it a fucking premonition. We locked eyes as he slid his big dick inside of me. I tried to catch my breath and I saw the pleasure he was getting out of me gripping the sheets at the feeling of him entering me.

"Oh my gosh." I cried out as he fell closer to me and wrapped my legs around his waist. I let my legs dangle over his ass as I felt his hips thrusting deeper and deeper inside of me.

"Shit, baby. You're tight as hell." He said in disbelief. His dick filled every nook and cranny my pussy had. I cocked my legs open wide and put my finger directly on my clit. I'd satisfied the craving of him filling me up; now I just needed to satisfy my throbbing clit.

"Fuck me, baby." I softly said, prompting him to go deeper inside of me. I gripped his dick with my walls and I heard him whimper as I squeezed and released, squeezed and released.

Zeus pinned my legs back and pressed down deeper inside of my hole. I wanted to scream in pleasure, but I needed him to keep going. I didn't need a scream, a yell or a noise to throw him off. I couldn't believe I felt like I was going to cum again. This had never happened. Before I knew it, Zeus was lifting my legs over his shoulders and was fucking the shit out of me. My head got closer and closer to the headboard as my body got closer and closer to climax. Zeus looked down on me and I quickly pulled his face down to mine and placed my tongue deeply into his mouth. I heard our combined juices slapping together, further turning me on. In one swift motion, Zeus had pulled back from our kiss and pulled my toes to his mouth. One by one he sucked each toe and I opened my mouth in pleasure as I watched him devour my toes. I had never had my toes sucked, so my pussy was gushing while he slid his tongue in and out of my freshly pedicured toes. I probably had already came on his dick while he intensely tongue-fucked my feet, but I wanted more of him and in different positions.

"Let me ride you." I begged as he fell back with a satisfied grin plastered on his face.

"I've been wanting to see that ass bounce on my dick since I first laid eyes on you." He said deviously.

I grabbed the headboard with my free hand and I slid him inside of me. I arched my back and allowed my ass to surround his dick. Feeling his dick hit the inside of my walls from this position had me ready to call the cops. This had to be illegal. I locked my legs behind his and got myself into the perfect riding position and rolled my hips as I took him in and out of me. I felt in control of the situation and took him gripping my hips as a sign that he was okay with that. I sped my rhythm up as I felt Zeus slapping my ass and guiding me with his hands. My ass was in his hands as he forcefully lifted and pushed my ass down on his dick. I followed his lead and arched my ass high in the air and swiftly brought it down on his dick. I heard my ass hitting his thighs and heard him moan loudly.

"Ride that dick, baby!" He yelled as he wrapped his arms around my waist and matched my rhythm and fucked me back. Fuck Tae-bo or Zumba, Zeus was all the cardio I needed. I continued popping my ass on him, making sure to give him the ride of his life.

"Get on all fours." He whispered in my ear before nibbling on it.

I did as I was told and watched over my shoulder as Zeus admired my ass poking out in the air. I'd learned the importance of arching my back, especially during doggy-style.

"Look at that pretty ass." Zeus said as he shook his head, before entering me.

I placed my head in the pillow and moaned loudly, as I felt him penetrate me. I could feel my ass jiggling everywhere as Zeus gripped my waist and pulled me into him. I met his pace and made sure to add my own spice to it. I pushed back on his dick so that I was, essentially, riding him and controlling the pace until I felt Zeus melt into me. Our sweaty bodies were one and it was a weird feeling of oneness. I could feel Zeus' speed picking up as he gripped me tighter and dug deeper into me. I felt his balls slapping against my ass and knew this was what real fucking was all about. I reached between my legs and played with my pussy and his balls at the same time.

"It's something about your sexy ass, Georgia. I don't know what it is." Zeus said as he flipped me over on my back and entered me with my legs straight up in the air.

Zeus picked up one of my breasts, put it in his mouth and closed his mouth as he slowly, and then quickly, fucked me roughly. He moaned as I watched him roll his eyes into the back of his head and fuck me with such intensity it scared me. I watched as my titties bounced all over the place and spread my legs widely to allow Zeus all the room he needed to get to his treasure.

"Shit, baby. Shit Georgia." Zeus whined loudly as he struggled to get his sentences and his strokes out.

In no time, Zeus had pulled his dick out of me, ripped the condom off and was standing over me jacking his dick. In most instances, I wouldn't have been keen on being fucked and came ON, but Zeus had tasted so delicious earlier that I was fiening for more of his sticky, tasty cum. I took his balls in my mouth again and made sure to swirl them around quickly, causing Zeus's toes to pop again. I watched closely as he grabbed my breasts and closed his eyes tightly before yelling loudly.

"SHIT!" He screamed as cum spewed everywhere. I scrambled to catch every drop that came from him. I'm sure I looked like a zoned out crackhead, trying to get the last of the free crack; but I didn't care. This was my dick. This was my cum. I wanted it all; by any means necessary.

I licked my fingers as I devoured the remnants of his cum that had landed on my fingers.

"Shit, girl." Zeus said, grabbing my face and kissing me like I was the woman of his dreams. In my mind, I told myself that we'd had something special; even if it was a damn lie.

I rolled over in the bed and headed to the shower. I grinned widely as I stepped into the warm shower and lathered up the sudsy rag as I wiped my entire body down.

"You mind if I join you?" I heard Zeus ask as he pulled the glass shower door back and stepped in.

I bit my bottom lip in excitement and before I could even object or oblige, I watched Zeus get on his knees. The water fell on to his head and back; he dug his face into my pussy like he couldn't fathom the thought of being away from it. I gripped the steel bars in the shower and gasped as I tried to remember how I could stand being apart from Zeus's tongue. I was already sensitive and it didn't help when he engulfed all of my pussy in his mouth and began sucking on it like a Popsicle on a hot Summer's day. He lifted my leg on top of his shoulder and dug his face in there deeper. I couldn't tell if he just enjoyed eating my pussy or if he was looking for something up there. I know time hadn't gone by that quickly, but I felt my leg getting weak as I pushed his head to the point of no return as I grinded everything I had into his face.

"You taste so good, baby." Zeus said pulling his face from between my legs. My freshly waxed pussy needed him there. I pushed his head back between my legs and prepared myself to cum again. I braced myself on Zeus' body and the steel bars as I tried to catch my breath.

As I dried off, I tried not to think about the fact that this could be the one and only time I had this perfect pussy eater and dick slinger in my presence. Zeus washed his face and brushed his teeth as I wrapped myself in the white, damp covers and headed to the window overlooking downtown Atlanta.

I must have been daydreaming when Zeus came behind me, stark naked, and placed his body on mine. He wrapped his hands around my waist and motioned for me to fall back into his chest. I listened to his heart beat and sighed.

"Did you know this was going to happen when you came to the concert?" Zeus asked, breaking our silence. I felt his dick getting hard as it sat near my ass and I was ready for more fucking, not more questioning.

"Of course not." I said picking his hand up and kissing it softly. "I didn't even know if you'd like me when we met."

"It's something about you Georgia." Zeus repeated as he kissed my shoulder blade and continued his tongue up to my ear.

"I'm sure you tell every girl, in every city, that." I said forcing a smile on my face.

The truth was, I wanted to believe that I was the only one who had fucked him like there was no tomorrow or yesterday.

Zeus turned me around and planted a kiss so passionate on me, all I could do was fall in to him. He grabbed my hand and led me back to the bed where I was sure we were about to pick up round three. When Zeus cuddled up behind me and didn't make a move, I didn't know what to think.

"How'd you get your name?" He asked pulling me closer to him. This was the shit movies were made of, not one-night stands with international superstars.

I cleared my throat and took a deep breath.

"My dad was born and raised in Georgia and loved it here." I said as I felt Zeus's hands roaming up and down my body. "When he married my mom, they relocated to Florida and he always said he would give anything to go back to Georgia." I said.

"When they had me. I was the easiest tribute he could pay to Georgia."

"You know I was born and raised here, too, right?"

Of course I'd known that. Hell, I'd read plenty of interviews with him telling that same piece of information; however, I let him continue.

"I think I remember seeing that somewhere." I said stroking his hand, which was resting on top of my stomach.

"I've got to say, this is the best taste of Georgia I've ever had." Zeus said with a reflective grin.

I should have felt bad about fucking a married man, but I didn't. Blame my satisfied pussy or the fact that I was actually attaching myself to the words this man was whispering in my ear. Each line could have been complete bullshit, but I didn't care. If—for only that night—I wanted to think Zeus gave a fuck about who he was fucking.

I closed my eyes and felt sleep coming over me, just as Anthony Hamilton's, "The Point of It All" began playing from his iPad and pulled his arms closer in to me.

Zeus began planting kisses on my shoulder blade and let his lips take him to the cusp of my ass and began circling his tongue delicately on my plump ass cheeks.

"Get on all fours." He demanded. As usual, I did as I was told.

I watched over my shoulder as Zeus laid flat on his back.

"Sit on my face. I want to make sure I keep the taste of Georgia with me."

I lowered my pussy on to his beautiful face and tingled as I felt his tongue hit my clit. This had to be a dream. This man didn't just like to eat pussy, he loved it. He cupped my ass while he pushed his head deeper as I rode his face like I'd ridden his dick. I listened to Anthony Hamilton croon as my body came over and over again. I clasped my hands together with Zeus's as he gripped my hips and pulled my body closer to his face.

We fell asleep together in other's arms that night. I know that sounds cliche, but it's true. My head fell against his chiseled chest and his arms wrapped around my waist.

"Please don't forget about me." I said softly once I heard him starting to pick up a slight snore.

That next morning, I woke up and gave Zeus the best morning head I'd ever given, before we both fell asleep again. I felt soft kisses all over my face shortly after and opened my eyes to see him putting on a t-shirt.

"I've got to go. I've got some interviews." Zeus said as he

leaned in to my face and sucked my lips.

I pulled his face closer to mine.

"Remember. Don't forget me." I said looking in to his eyes for an ounce of genuineness.

"I won't Georgia. Believe me." He said kissing my lips softly one more time. "Now get you some more rest."

I closed my eyes tightly and hoped that when I opened my eyes that dick and those lips would be next to me. I wasn't holding out hope, though.

***

"I need to get my car out of valet." I said pulling my ticket from my purse and handing it to the front desk receptionist. I'd given up on the search for the gold lamè thong panties.

The young, twenty-something girl entered my ticket number, glanced up at me and smiled.

"Were you in 222 with Mr. Anderson?"

My face flushed red as I dropped my head and nodded "yes." There I was, my hair looking like a mess, my panties nowhere to be found and the receptionist was seeing me do the "walk of shame."

"He left this for you." She said handing me an over-sized manila envelope. "Your car should be pulling up at any minute."

I calmly walked my panty-less ass out of the hotel and slid the valet $20 and got into my car and pulled off. I turned into a gas station as I neared my apartment and finally let my curiosity get the best of me as I tore into the envelope.

Out dropped my gold lamè thong panties and a handwritten note.

I gripped the panties in one hand and grinned while reading the short note.

"I'll never forget the Taste of Georgia that you gave me.

Thank you.

Love,

Zeus

P.S. Check your text messages."

I giggled to myself and pushed my hair behind my ear as I scrambled to check my texts; sure enough, Zeus had already sent me one that read: "I ENJOYED YOUR COMPANY LAST NIGHT. I WILL NOT FORGET YOU. THANK YOU. Z."

Just as I read the text message for the fourth time and giggled, my phone began buzzing. It was Sandra.

I answered coolly.

"So how was last night? What you'd end up doing?" She said with a yawn, "I bet you made another loaf of banana nut bread, huh?"

I grinned widely as I thought about rubbing my night of a life in her face.

"Yeah, I did. And you know what? I think I've found the secret to making my bread rise."

Sandra took a deep breath. "You're so vanilla, Georgia."

"Oh well." I smiled as I laughed to myself while I pulled out of the gas station with my gold lamè panties, a wet pussy and a secret I'd take to the grave with me.

I wasn't vanilla Georgia anymore. My one night with Zeus had granted me a chance to experience the delightful effect that the taste of Georgia had.

Strawberry ice cream, anyone?

Nights over Egypt

By
Elissa Gabrielle

"The sexual heat that rests between two forbidden souls can become so intense that a combustion ensues when desires are met." ~Egypt

Divinity and Purgatory

Her...

He's the kind of man that makes you love your name, just because the words part so sensually from his delicious lips. "King," that's his name and it fits him like a hand in glove. You see, he is regal, superior in human form, aesthetically – he has been blessed with more than his fair share.

The blink of an eye seems like an eternity while enveloped in his embrace. Hot, heavy sounds of getting off, his breath came out on an emanation of satisfaction that filled the atmosphere. Constant coos controlled the congo-like tempo equating to the fragile sounds of an inner shame. I'm embarrassed about the way I've freaked. Nothing should be this damn good. It is a sin and a divine shame for anything to be this glorious.

An ebony towering inferno, locked in dreads; he is divinity and purgatory all rolled into one masterful man of perfection.

Quite frankly, my goal is to make him wetter than he's ever been...

How long can you handle this?" he smiled, flashing a set of grand piano keys in the process. Sweat poured from his chocolate skin like flowing waterfalls. Have mercy, I thought. Chocolate makes everything better.

"Until one of us cries for mercy," I replied, smiling, staring at his God-like presence. I must have died and gone to heaven, even though, I'm more than convinced that nothing this delightful could even take place in the house of the Lord.

We enjoyed the luxury of not knowing one another too well, so we had to guess each other's favorite fragrance; had to take a stab at what each one of us deserved.

Like a string of warm chocolate pieces leading and lighting the path to a romantic lover's bedroom, his spirit knows the way into my inner sanctum and with the auspicious praise of the righteous, his body gathers in solemn assembly, as his confident heart speaks to my throne alone. The majestic offering of his love carpets the pathway to my virtuous destiny, and it pleases, in every sense of the word.

Living in a fantasy, he became my "baby," infinitely, and I became his favorite flavor, laced in triple D cups. He is teaching me all the dirty sounds of love.

"This is the best pussy I've ever had. You know that, right?"

In the Beginning...

Him...

It was the light of her smile. It spoke to me in a way no other woman had. It was like sunshine on the most dreary of days; lighting up my heart and my mind. Simply, her smile. Her smile somehow said to me, "Baby, one day, I'll be all yours." At least that's what my foolish heart wanted to believe.

Was it so familiar how soft she called my name?

Egypt blossomed right before my eyes over a period of months, maybe a year even, before I found the courage to approach her. I had seen her at "Nights," a popular poetry, grown and sexy nightclub downtown Newark. The bricks were live on Friday nights.

I'll never forget the night I saw her for the first time. She walked in, bold, brilliant, like a goddess she appeared, tall, thick, voluptuous, flowing hair that caressed her shoulders effortlessly. She held a set of bouncing, beautiful breasts that screamed for attention. I watched her every move that night. From the form-fitting black tee with the word "Savior" etched in silver she rocked to the denim that had the pleasure of holding and hugging those honey-sweet thighs; I jocked her, no question.

Lips as soft as cotton, brushed with some hot cherry-red color shined, even from half a room away. The almond shaped eyes were mesmerizing from afar, and as she batted her lashes and glanced in my direction, she threw me a smile...yes, I knew that smirk was for me.

Now, so many thoughts ran like a marathon through my mind, daily, weekly, monthly; every minute, every hour, I'm consumed with dreams of her. It's only been a year since our eyes met, since her inception into my world; a lonely world where vultures and thieves threaten to steal her away from me. One year, since I've met the love of my life, the reason for my existence. One year, since I've neared Heaven, almost kissed an angel, tasted the sweetness of innocence. If wanting her this badly is wrong, then I can't ever be right. At night, I see her in my dreams, and by day, I'm mesmerized.

The windows to my soul close softly. And, after doing so, I drift off into a world where only she and I exist. A lustful land of lovely love-making is where I lay my head nightly. It is a delicious deserted desolate place where desires of the heart dwell and decadence reign supreme.

From the beginning, I needed her...

"King," man, you're up brother. Julius took me out of my memorization with her and notified me of my time to shine on stage. Friday nights, open mic, and me, not only is "King," my name, it's a word that I tend to live by. I'm a grown-ass man. I put away childish things quite some time ago.

"Alright, alright," I replied, put down my Crown Royal on ice, pulled my dreads back into a string and made my way to the stage. Bright lights beamed on me as I took the last three steps up to meet the microphone; I call her—the microphone— Lily, and she accompanies me each and every Friday night.

The cello player, Rob, works the chords, sloo-footed and all and my mans 'anem on the bass, drums and sax join me. This stuff right here, this galaxy that I drift off into is never rehearsed, it simply comes from the dome, through my spirit, parts from my lips, lands on Lily who distributes me to the audience.

My right hand covers the top of my brow as I try to shield the lights, in hopes of finding perfection in its purest form. Back then I didn't know her name. But I'm searching for her. I want what I have to say to reach her and I plan to try harder than Avis to make sure she knows that my thoughts are solely on her and her alone. Yes, there are plenty of good looking women in here, but I know what I like. I know what I want. And you better believe, I know what I need.

"Alright, alright. How's everyone in the house tonight?"

The crowd replies with whistles and light tapping sounds. I see candles lit all around. I smell vanilla, cognac and cigars in the air. I see lighters up and drinks everywhere. I see her, my queen, she's right over there.

"Are you ready for some words that will intoxicate your mind? Send you to a place you haven't gone before? Say word?"

"Word!" I hear them. I see them all. Lovely looking mamacitas, brothers dressed to the nines, and her...I see my Queen. She smiles. I feel my blood racing through my veins. She's the fuel I need to turn this motherfucker out.

"You wearing that button-up, baby!" A random chick screams. I smile.

"Thank you, baby."

The bass moves throughout the club and although no one says a word, we all have an understanding that things change from this point on. We all know our roles; witnesses and stars, voyeurs and spectators, folks mesmerized by the words, to poetry-junkies and groupies or simply folks who want and need to have a good time. We all are at attention, unspoken rules, we play our positions...me up first to bat.

"I call this one Savior," I speak softly into Lily. She receives me, distributes me fluently throughout the room. I close my eyes and flow.

"She appeared out of the night sky.
Pleasing.
Tantalizing to my eyes.
Emperor.
Warrior.
Goddess.
The sweet smell of lust.
The soft strains of love.
I bowed at her feet.
Kissed them.
My Queen.

With all praise due to the most high,
My savior, can you feel the roar of my stare?
As I become familiar with those naughty parts of you that
Seductively hide under the clothes you're forced to wear.
I dare.
Salaciously, I praise you.
Spirit to spirit.
Body and soul.
I want you.
Tell me that you want me too.

Picture this...

Finger up, tip-toeing to your alter.

Call out your name.

Liberate you as the tip of my nose brushes against the thick, sugary lips

You hold so sacred.

I take full blame.

Let me make it my daily bread.

To partake in, over and over again.

Let me make the erotic heaven of your lonely earth sing.

Precious savior.

Delicious queen.

Cool off the fire of my wanting.

Extinguish the bountifulness of my heat.

Help me to resolve my condition.

One day I will drink in the mainstream of your mind.

Let me get lost in your holy ocean.

Baptize me into complete submission.

Savior…"

Plenty dap as I make my way off the stage. Few honey-dips trying to holler, but my mind is in a place and time where my world with my queen is perfect. Politely, I excuse myself from the swarm and take my seat – my usual throne, corner side booth, with Julius, my boy from around the way.

"Dope, brother, as usual. Seemed a lil personal though."

"It was," I point to her as she makes her way to the stage.

"I see." Julius smiles, shakes his head, takes a sip of the dark drink that will mess with his mind soon.

Truth be told, I don't even think she knows my name. As I sit here, the midnight clear greets me in isolation and desperation, yearning for penetration as my right hand presses against the chocolate-coated staff that beats and pulsates in anticipation of her. Julius has left the booth, which gives me time to fantasize. Gradually, my eyes open, and the animal inside of me has been awakened by that thing – Lust. The creature in me is begging for the gentleman in me to get the fuck out of the way so that I can hunt and capture my prey.

Staring at the purple colored bar in my Friday lion's den, my eyes close once more, and I envision her beauty again. If I lose sight of her, even if only in my dreams, I'm afraid my heart would not only break; the fear of not having something I crave more than life itself, will force me into psychosis.

Damn, I need her...

Her stride, how she glides, her walk, in rhythm to the Earth's beat, she moves with fluidity...like if perfection could be transformed and placed in human form -perfectly planted on a man's heart, walking, simply walking, and I am in awe.

From her toffee-colored, rich butter soft, butterscotch skin, to the flowing brown hair that shines and cascades, framing a face that the Gods took extra time to create, to her deep-pitted dimple in her right cheek, to her radiant smile, this woman has everything I've ever prayed for. I've only known of her physical existence for a short time, but she's been in my soul, in my thoughts and dreams, a part of my nightly talks with God, for most of my adult life. I've found her.

Deliciousness dares me to deliberately devour all that is so divine about her. What I'd give to taste the tender goodness that sits between her thighs. If only for one night, I'd taste the tantalizing, tempting, treasure, that tickles my fancy, night after night.

Her name is Egypt.

Heaven and Hell

Her...

His name is King. That much I do know. He is a serious combination of both Heaven and Hell, good and evil, hot and ice cold, a towering inferno of rich dark chocolate adorned in frosty brown dreadlocks.

He's so fly that he walks in slow motion-the confidence in his stride, that Denzel-like strut in his oh so sexy swagger convinces me that my immediate assumption may be right-his dick does effortlessly flow to his knees. My God.

Cocoa-dipped passion in male form. Whenever I see him, I try not to blink so that I won't miss a goddamn thing.

He has to be around six foot three, and I know his body is hard as rocks. I can see it through his purple button-up.

To say that I want him would probably be the understatement of the year. I know what I like. I know what I want. And I definitely know what I need. I need him is a more accurate description of my true feelings.

I long for King at night, right before I lay my burdens down. My longing transcends into that galaxy of the unknown, in my sleep where my dreams reveal all of my life's fears and desires, and he represents an equal part of both. Thoughts of him travel with me throughout my day, and I often take him to places he shouldn't dare go. I'm ashamed of where's he's been in my world, on my list of life's goals and priorities. In my dreams, he has yet to remain. He has effortlessly and deliberately become a permanent fixture in my fantasy and reality.

The two of them often collide.

Trying to pinpoint the time I first saw his delicious ass is hard, but I know he hasn't left my heart since that first day. It was a day, just like today, where I go to find peace of mind, solace, an escape from the ordinary, and delve into rhythm and rhyme at "Nights," in Newark.

"Nights..." a place where true talent reigns supreme. Soldiers of the pen gather to pay homage to one of the greatest gifts we have, the gift of the written word. A place where masterful spoken word tyrants come to duke it out on stage, trying to see whose word game is untouchable for the evening. None of these cats admit it's a competition, but the audience can see the fire in each and every one of their eyes as they spit verse after verse, hoping that their crescendo escalates to the point of no return.

This is where King leads all, and those who know the truth, follow. His words, week after week, flow majestically from his sweet, dark chocolate lips, and pour fluidly from his mouth, and somehow goes straight to my heart, travels to my breasts, erects my nipples, lands on my clit, and beats the shit, hell and damn out of my pussy walls.

There have been many nights where I watched King spit

fire. Many nights, I captured his flame and took it home with me. So hot...my panties were soaked with the remnants of my longing.

He's just left the stage. Roars and applause from brothers and sisters alike. I can see his smile, his pride, its slight, he holds it in to remain humble, I can tell. I know my baby that well.

Delirium has officially set in. I welcome it. Means I'm on some path that leads to him, no matter how irrational.

I see him. That strut. I see that track star behind, tight, round, moving in sync with the momentum of his poetic victory. Walk that walk, money. I want to run up behind him, hug him with all that I own in my spirit, gently kiss the back of his neck, and delicately whisper in his ear, "Good job, baby." I'd be showing these groupie-stank-ass-slut-bitches in here, who fawn over his delightful self, that he is mine...alone.

Wear that shirt, honey. Those denims are hugging you in all the right places...damn. I watch as brothers give him dap and respect and love. Disgusted, I see the ladies give him love too. The kind of love I want to give him. The kind of love he deserves and the kind of love I know he's worthy of.

He spoke about a Savior in a way I'd never heard before. As my mind shifts in high gear to fantasy realm, I can only hope that he was referring to me. As with anything in real life, sometimes truth is indeed stranger than fiction and on some days makes fiction look as sane as Obama. However, with the way real life works, I know he couldn't possibly have been referring to me. Not sure if the heavens would work so highly in my favor, all at the same time, to invoke some divine influence on the possible unofficial meeting of two kindred yet unfamiliar souls.

I remember him saying, "Let me make the erotic heaven

of your lonely earth sing. Precious savior. Delicious queen."
The way he puts words together is like magic and not everyone
can do it.

Not everyone...but I sure can. I walk towards the stage,
and my eyes follow King until he disappears as the spotlight
greets me, makes me turn into another soul, one who is here to
deliver lyrical enlightenment on a crowd of kings and queens
who need to be uplifted and transported to a place unfamiliar
and not yet known to them. I will do that. Encourage, enlighten,
maybe even inspire, with a twist. Tonight, I'm not starring in
the role of poor righteous teacher. I'm going to speak to my
man, and pray that I don't make a fool of myself. Hope beyond
hope that he's listening. I'm going to speak to King, as if, by
the slightest chance, and the slimmest ray of hope that he did
lay it out on the line for me just a short time ago.

I nod at the bass player and sit my drink on the stool
next to me. I have no clue as to what I will say, but I know
that the words will come to my spirit, and come to my mind
and be delivered from the heart and soul as they should be.
Understanding the power of words, I get what this moment
means. My life depends on this very moment.

"My people. What's good?"

"You girl," a gentleman with a gap between his teeth yells
from the front row.

"I like that, Papi." I smile.

"I call this piece, "Denomination."

"I watch you as you sleep.

Too comfortable to face it.

That you make my life complete.

And I've yet to know your last name.

Wanna trace it.

I rebel.

While today is still today,
I need to choose well.

Ain't picked up a bible in years.
Yet, I know your presence flows
through the space of heavenly design.
Christen my condition with your tears.

The word revealed.
They will never again be hungry or thirsty.
They will never be scorched by the heat of the sun.
With your heavenly heat
Melt down the walls of my inhibition
And denominate me as your only one.

The lust of my flesh.
The lust of my eyes.
The pride of my life.
Won't keep me from getting to heaven.
I'll just proclaim that a King,
A man,
Who is worthy of the name,
Reigned down on me,
With the sacred fist of the righteous,
And made my world sane.
King."

Butterflies threaten to take complete control of every inch of my body but I am not a punk and I won't be bitching out of this situation. Red-faced and all, I said it, I now own it. Worst case scenario, he rejects me, even if he paid attention at all, life goes on and I tuck my stupid-ass tail between my legs and make it out the front door with the swiftness. Best case is that my love heard, received and digested everything I said to him and he'll take me home soon to meet his Mama.

A girl can dream.

As I exit the stage, many of the weekly visitors and familiar faces greet me with joy and love and excitement and I take it all in, although the only thing on my mind is him. As I walk down the stairs, I feel all of the fullness of my breasts as they bounce, my nipples harden in anticipation of him. I don't see him anywhere.

Making my way to the bar, I sit on an empty stool and speak to Renee, a long-time friend and bartender here at "Nights."

She smiles. "Honey, that was good and different for you."

"Thank you, darling."

"Your usual?"

"Yes, Ma, you know me so well. Brandy Alexander."

"You got it."

I watch Renee as she makes her way to the other side of the bar. She knows I prefer to drink out of glasses with a pencil thin rim, so she pulls out the finest for her girl.

I feel him.

He's here.

His presence is domineering.

I glance to my right, and my peripheral captures his silhouette. King. King. King. Damn. King. Heart rate climbing. Breathe easy. Exhale. It's going to be alright, baby girl. Lord, have mercy. Okay. Make sure your tits are sitting up straight. Arch your back, bitch. Man up. Put your big girl panties on.

He takes the stool next to me. I don't look in his direction. His cologne has the power to make me drop to my knees.

"What it is, Renee?" He questions the bartender as he sits.

She hands me my drink. "Here you go, Egypt."

"Thanks," I whisper under a nervous tremble of my voice.

"Egypt, it is, eh?" King remarks.

Silence.

Renee laughs out loud. "Silly woman, King is talking to you."

"Oh," I chuckle, turn towards him. Damn, his eyes. I'm going to wet my panties in five, four, three, two, one...

"Yes, it's Egypt. Nice to meet you, King."

"Oh, you know the name, eh?" He smiles. Waves his hand to Renee.

"Renee, I'll have what Egypt is having."

"Coming right up, boss."

"Thanks, sweetie."

My eyes gravitate to his chiseled, manly face. He is a beautiful, black man. Beautiful.

"I do know your name." I smile.

"I'm honored." He moves in closer to me. The perfectly trimmed goatee looked delicious from afar, but up close and personal, it looks like heaven..

"Why is that?"

"This world is so cold and ugly, that its refreshing to have someone as lovely as you remember something so important about me." He smiles.

Just breathe.

An unstable chuckle leaves me.

"You are beautiful, Egypt."

"Thank you, King."

He moves in closer. The space, the heat that rests between us is palpable, ignitable.

King takes strands of my hair from my face with his left hand and gently brushes them back.

My nipples harden.

"Loved your piece, Egypt."

"Thank you, King. I loved yours also. Skillful how you incorporated biblical elements. I take my hat off to you, sir."

"Just your hat?" He smiles. Takes a sip of his drink.

"For now," I reply.

"Well, praise the Lord, there's hope for me, yet."

"Keep praising."

"Ha, ha, ha. You're adorable, Egypt."

"As are you, King."

I glance at my watch and figure I'd end this on a high note. Because if I stay any longer, and any more of this liquid aphrodisiac enters my bloodstream, I will, without a doubt, be sitting on King's face tonight.

"Well, nice meeting you, King. I'm out of here. "

"You know my days and nights are going to be a living hell until the next time I see your glorious face." He smiles, takes another sip. My eyes peer to his feet, and travel up his legs, to his abdomen, chest, his strong neck, broad shoulders, and land on his sweet, delectable lips. Wow, what I'd give up to kiss them, just one time.

Boldly, I take King's hand in mine, pull the pen from the bar, and write my telephone number into his palm.

"Call me, anytime."

"It's like that?"

"It's like that, King...Later."

I know he's watching me as I exit...have mercy.

To Have Dominion

Her...

I made it home, via Cloud 9, as I soared through the inner workings of a ghetto, on a wing and a prayer with thoughts of King who consumed my mind. Don't even remember what route I took to get here, but thankful that I made it home safely.

An overwhelming sexiness covers me as I make my way to the shower. Peeling off layers of clothing, they drop to the floor, along with any cares I've carried with me for the day. Nothing even matters right now, but the warmth of black vanilla bubbles as they cascade down my back.

I can't believe we spoke this evening. What a pleasure to behold all that is good and worthy and precious about him up close, live and direct, in physical form. He's more delightful than I ever imagined he could be. That tiny chuckle he let escape him lets me know that there's greater laughs to be had with my man. I sense he has a very silly streak in him. Can't wait to learn more.

My loofa gently glides over parts of my body that need to be cleansed. If only they had a loofa for the mind, I would be able to scrub away these naughty thoughts and inappropriate fantasies that consume me. I watch as the scented, soft soap runs down my chest, and in between my breasts. Taking the loofa, I softly brush my nipples as I watch them grow right before my eyes.

I remember him...King. I remember his smile. The way he touched my hair. I remember his laugh. I think of him. I long for him. I want him. I need him. Oooh, I taste him. I touch him. I kiss him. Oh God, I devour him. Get on all fours for him. King. I catch his thrust, give it right back to him. Give him my tongue. Taste his lips. I'm squirting love all over him. Enjoying his tongue tricks. Damn, he's pulling my trigger.

The phone rings. Nothing disturbs this groove.

My hands travel down my abdomen. Finger tips run across my navel, down to the center of my longing. My face receives the hot beads of water. I think of him. My King. My baby. My mind is half crazy. Dreams won't leave him alone. I remember him. He said it. Spoke to me. Kissed my soul. Made love to my mind. Ravaged me with his words. Let the world into his desire. Made me a spectacle, just for me. He mouthed the words . Oh God. "With all praise due to the most high, My savior, can you feel the roar of my stare? As I become familiar with those naughty parts of you that seductively hide under the clothes you're forced to wear."

It's raining over here, on the inside of my womb. I need him. King. Come. Cool down the fire of my wanting. Hands travel down to a place that's been waiting an eternity for King to touch. I'm his woman. His for the taking. Sweet, syrupy juices cover my fingers as I make myself familiar with King's clit. I'm running my tongue across my lips, wetting them, while wishing he was here. Shit, he's making my pussy sing a new song.

I see him. King. Outlining my nipples with his tongue. He's in me now. My sugary, hot volcano welcomes him. Anxiously, they make a place for him to stay. He has a new home. His tempered thrusts are enough to cause an eruption between my thighs. I yell for him. Reach for him. He's not here, but he is here, pleasing me. "King," I call him as I release. His loving runs down my thighs. Throbbing. Set ablaze. Skin too hot to touch. On fire. King. I remember you. The air in the room is blanketed with the aroma of sex. A collision of lust and hunger makes me explode.

Lightning and thunder. I'm on my way. In the worst kind of way. Lightning strikes. My storm is raging. Won't let go. I never seen it, but I found this love, I wanna feel it. I feel him. I happily give him sweet cherries from my lips, grapes off of my vine, pearls from my mind, diamonds from my womb and rolling thunder from my hips. King.

Damn...

Stretched out across my bed, I exhale as I relive it all. My encounter with my favorite nightmare. Lincoln Jazz Center Orchestra's "Jelly, Jelly," plays softly in the background. I flip over to my belly, grab my phone. The red light is blinking. Voicemail. I retrieve it.

"You have one new message. To listen to the message, press one."

I press the number one on my phone, place the phone on speaker. Lay the phone down next to me on the bed.

"Sweet, beautiful woman. You didn't give me enough time with you this evening. And, I didn't give you my number. I guess that's why I'm going into voicemail now. Anywho, just wanted to hear your lovely voice. Wanted to grab a little bit of your energy. Hit me back, when you can, at 862-555-1612. Have a restful night, baby."

Have mercy. King. Called. Me. My heart flutters as I try to gather my thoughts. It's one o'clock in the morning. Should I return his call? It's too late isn't it? Don't want to be rude.

A clicking sound comes from my phone and I check the screen to see what action lies ahead. I have a new text message. Clicking on the envelope, I can't help but wonder who it is.

Message from 862-555-1612 at 1:14 a.m: "Sorry I missed you. It's King. Would love to hear your voice."

He's bold. Beautiful. He's bold and beautiful and lovely and black and regal and damn...I'm returning this text. I save his number and label it "King."

Me: I'm sorry you missed me, too. ☺

King: Is that right?

Me: Yes, Sir.

King: I like your formality.

Me: Do you?

King: I like you. ☺

Me: Music to my ears.

King: Why is that?

Me: Because I kinda sorta like you too. ☺

King: Confusion, Queen?

Me: No, just kidding. It is 1 a.m. ☺

King: Aww, does the baby need to go to sleep?

Me: Ha, ha. No, I'm good.

King: You are.

Me: I am, what?

King: Good.

Me: How would you know?

King: Because I've felt your presence. Your spirit overflows with all that is good.

Me: I like the way that sounds.

King: Me too. LOL

Me: You're funny.

King: Thank you, baby.

Me: You're welcome.

King: Would love to see you again.

Me: I would like that. I'll be at Night's on Friday.

King: Too long to wait. Come to Night's tomorrow. They're having live jazz. 7pm.

Me: Hmmm.

King: Hmmm, what?

Me: You're dangerous.

King: I'm not going to kill you. ☺

Me: LOL.

King: No need to be afraid. Jazz. Good convo. Dinner. That's it.

Me: See you tomorrow, King.

King: That's it? No kiss? No, hugs? Nothing?

Me: Muah. Is that better?

King.   Much. I'll hold onto this until tomorrow. You'll give me the real one, tomorrow right?

Me: Time will tell. Have a good night, King.

King: You too, gorgeous. ☺

In a Sentimental Mood

Him...

Somehow I'm not satisfied. I mean, I'll see Egypt soon enough, but this last text from her is not enough to get me through the night. I look at the phone again. It reads, "Time will tell.

Have a good night, King." Damn, I need more of her. I lay in this cold, lonely bed. Just me, alone, with my thoughts, dark room, the moon piercing through my blinds. Shines a light on my body. My nature rises. I see it grow underneath soft, charcoal-colored sheets. Coltrane plays intensely throughout my bedroom. His sax game encourages me to act on impulse, just the way that horn does when he plays; an intensely emotional force overwhelms me.

Black boxer briefs are the only thing getting in the way of me and my rod. If I don't get her off of my mind, something is going to have to be done, and soon. Pre-come starts to leak from the tip and I feel the urge to be inside of her. I know that pussy is incredible. My right hand finds its way to my right thigh. I'm tempted. Need to hear her voice. Can't call. Its too late. I wonder what she's doing over there?

The rainy-snow mixture pours fluidly outside, making musical notes and dances its own jig this evening. It's cold, so cold outside, and my heart, like a homeless man in this dreary weather, needs shelter, comforting and loving. I miss my woman, Egypt, and she's not even my woman, yet I miss her. I miss her touch, and haven't touched her yet. I miss her smell, her smile, her laughter...and a night like tonight only emphasizes it more.

I close my eyes and dream of her...

Leaning over, I kiss her forehead and make my way down to her lips where I bite, lick and caress them ever so gently. Reaching her neck, she lets out the sexiest moan. Licking lightly then sucking strongly, my tongue has makes it way down to her breasts and I alternate between nipples. I get up.

Grabbing my shoulders, the look of fear overcomes her. "Baby, don't leave me now. I've been dreaming of being your whore. Please love me, Daddy."

Those tantalizing words ooze from her mouth, and enter my psyche, shooting orgasmic pulses through my entire being, finally landing at the tip of my length, where it releases my juices as I hunger for her even more.

"Shh, Baby, I'm not going anywhere. Take your shorts off and let me see that pretty pussy, please, baby."

Thick, caramelized thighs reach mid-air as she pulls off terrycloth shorts. Her meaty ass looks so good as her legs fall back to the bed. The fine hairs are just starting to grow back on her pussy, and her lips, now swollen with desire, scream, beg, silently for me to have a taste. Her pussy walls are imploring me to have my way with them, I just know it. Because, no one knows this pussy the way I do.

Back to reality. I grab the drink from my nightstand, take a sip. My hand touches my dick. I pull it out. Carefully, I stroke it. But its not enough. I need her.

Close my eyes again. I dream of her.

Reaching over, I place my finger in the glass of Bailey's, and my fingers roam to her nipples, where I smear the alcohol. My tongue slithers and drinks the libation from her. She's in desperate need of relaxation, and my needle will provide much needed acupuncture.

Her pretty face demands my attention, as our tongues dance with devil. Breathing is heavy. Her pants and moans make me want to finish this fantasy turned reality inside of her.

"Spread that pussy real nasty for me, Egypt," I command and she obliges.

I wake up once more. Fluid leaks more heavily. I use it as lubrication. My strokes are more aggressive. Fuck, I need to be inside of her.

My eyes close...again.

Head first, I dive into my feast, with gentle licks to hot pussy walls then move onto a swollen, bulbous clit which saturates my lips with slick, sweet, sap. Placing my fingers into her pretty hole, I move them in and out, round and round until orgasmic pulses shoot from her. Her body quivers.

Rubbing the juice onto my shaft, I get on top of her, and rub the tip vigorously onto her clit, she screams.

"Damn, baby, please don't make me wait anymore. Fuck me, King, please," she begs, I'm pleased.

With one blunt force impact, I'm deep inside the pussy I've grown to love. The look in her eyes confirms what I knew all along, that she loves me too, still. Rocking back and forth, in and out of her hot, slick, wet cave, makes her wetter and hotter with each stroke. The tightness holds me so damn good and with each dip, she digs puncture wounds into my back.

Oh, how she looks at me, when I'm deep inside-those eyes. Oh God, I would kill for those eyes.

I can't. I have to call her...

Pick up the phone, man up, I whisper to myself. I dial. I'm scared. She picks up. Damn, she sounds so sweet.

"Hello?" She speaks softly.

"Egypt?"

"Yes, King?"

"Uhm, what are you doing?" I let out a chuckle.

I can feel her smiling through the phone.

"I'm sleeping, baby. What are you doing, King?"

"Thinking about you, Egypt. You're so sweet." I'm almost there and she doesn't even know it.

"Is that right?"

"Yes," I moan.

"What were you thinking about, King?" She has the nerve to question me.

"You. Everything about you. You're so damn fine, Egypt," I whisper. I'm coming. I hope she can't here that.

"Sounds like I need to be there with you."

"You do."

"Soon, baby."

"Soon, what, beautiful?"

"Soon, you'll have me."

"I can't fucking wait."

"Nasty mouth, King. I like it."

"I like you, baby."

"I know, I can hear it, King..."

***

If I look at my watch one more time. Someone's gonna see me sweat. Never let them see you sweat. Can't let anyone in on my secret. After standing out here in the cold, waiting for my queen to arrive, I realize that she may not show up at all. It's seven-thirty. Nevertheless, I'll try to enjoy my evening. But damn, I was hoping she'd be able to catch a whiff of this new cologne, be privy to my latest button-up, new platinum around my neck, and , oh yes, this small token of affection I picked up for her earlier today. It's in my pocket, and If I had my way tonight, I'd give it to her, along with this long, thick dick that I'm more than confident she would love.

Making my way over to an empty table in the corner, I spot couples seated, sharing drinks and appetizers. I see folks already on the dance floor, jammin' to the tunes of live music.

The waitress comes over to take my order and reality slaps me in the face. I have no one to share this drink with. Well, plenty of women in here would love to, but that's how life works. The one you want is the only one you want and nothing else even matters.

"King, your usual?"

"No, Ma'am...let's change the pace a bit. I'll have a Brandy Alexander."

"Ooh, I like."

"Yeah, trying to step up my game a lil something, something." I smile. She walks off.

"Is this seat taken?" Ooooh chile, there goes my baby. I glance up and my eyes greet hers. A smile crosses her lips. My big ass kool aid smile takes up my entire face. I stand up, pull out her seat for her.

"This seat belongs to you, my dear." Standing behind Egypt, I move in close, remove her waist-length fur jacket. I can smell the scent of her hair. Freshly washed. Some type of melons or passion fruit or something delicious like that. I want to plant my face in her curls, inhale the sweet scent of my woman, but I choose to behave myself instead, offer her a seat.

"Thank you so much. Sorry I'm late. Traffic."

"No problem, baby. I would have waited all night." I tell her as I take my seat.

"You look great, King. Love the chain."

"You look even better, Egypt." She smiles. I want to kiss her.

The waitress returns with the drink. Places it in front of me. I tell her, "This is for my baby." Big smiles escape me. Egypt smiles, almost turns red. Graciously accepts the drink.

"Thank you, King."

"My pleasure, baby. Anything for you."

"Excuse me for breaking up this love affair, but King, should I bring your usual?" The waitress chuckles. I nod. She shakes her head, smiles, walks off, but not before whispering something into Egypt's ear. Egypt smiles. Damn, the chocolate lip gloss covers her lips the same way I want to. Makes me want a Hershey's kiss. Those piercing almond shaped eyes stare at me as she gets her girl-on-girl chuckle on, at my expense. Her lashes are so long, as she bats her eyes in my direction. Look at those dimples. Lord, help me. Those triple DDD's are sitting up, at attention, looking like they need order and direction. I love her form-fitting chocolate brown top. It shimmers when the light hits it.

She has the nerve to point in my direction. What the hell are they talking about? I gently grab her hand. I just want to touch her. Her hand is so soft. I kiss the back of it. Break up this lil high-school musical. I stand up, all while Egypt's hand is in mine. Tell the waitress that the conversation is over.

"Come on." I command and lead Egypt to the dance floor. She follows my lead. I like that about her. She's soft, bouncing her big, gorgeous ass behind me. I have a goddess on my arm, with me for the night. Egypt is, without question, a woman that every man wants, yet careful to desire.

The band covers Duke Ellington & John Coltrane's "In A Sentimental Mood." Taking Egypt into my arms, she doesn't resist, instead she falls into my warmth and my spirit. I'm comfortable having her in my embrace. She is so familiar to me. Like a soft strain of love.

Her hands cover both sides of my neck and my arms wrap around her waist. I lean in, place my face onto her shoulder, kiss it softly, inhale the sweet aroma that is her. I kiss her shoulder again as we rock side to side. Enjoying the horns and piano as they play a sweet melody made exclusively for us two. This is our night and our song, and our world is perfect. We don't say a word. I look in her eyes. She smiles.

Pulling her in closer. I need for Egypt to feel me. I want her to know that this ain't no game, that I'm not a joke. I don't want her ass, alone, I want her. I kiss her neck. She allows it. I feel her exhale. Oooh, the thoughts of kissing her turns into kissing her, fantasy meets reality, makes me high. I'm dizzy. She leans in, whispers in my right ear, "I love the way your lips feel." She brushes her face up against my cheek. She kisses my cheek. Pulls back. I move in closer, pull her to me. No more space for any more heat to fill. The space is gone. All taken up by two people, two spirits greeting, trying to become that one entity of love. I move in, kiss her cheek, whisper in her ear, "I'm a happy man tonight, Egypt. Thank you." I'm still in her ear, but I feel her smile, I feel her breathe-its staggered, like butterflies are fucking with her rhythm. She is gradually getting to a state I've been in for quite some time. Can't get right until it gets right.

I look in her eyes.

"You know I've been wanting you for so long." I kiss her forehead.

She gives me a sweet peck on my lips. She exhales a nervous puff of satisfaction when the man she had been longing for admitted that he needed her.

"Happy, because I've been wanting you even longer, King."

"Hungry?"

"For?" she smiles.

I rock her side to side. Laugh out loud. "Look at ya nasty ass. Are you hungry for food? Wanna eat?"

Embarrassed, she responds, "Yes."

We walk together, hand in hand and make our way back to our table.

Mellow jazz fills the air. The center of our table houses a crystal bowl filled with liquid and floating candles. A floor-length window allows for us to view the snow as it falls. We order our meals.

My queen plays with the rim of her drink with her fingertip. She circles it, grabs the glass. I touch her hand. Cover it with mine. She stiffens. Looks up to me. I move in closer to her.

"I like your hair." Taking my left hand, I brush dangling loose curls away from her face.

"What are we doing, King?"

"Making sure we don't miss this opportunity."

I continue to brush her hair. She takes a sip of her drink. Smiles, slightly.

"You wear those locks well." She leans in, softly caresses a few of them that hang onto my shoulder.

Taking the drink from her hand, I place the glass to my

lips. Take a sip.

"You like the way that tastes, King?"

"Yes."

"You kept kissing my shoulder."

"I've been thinking about that a lot."

I slide the drink back to my queen. Our food arrives. I stand up, take my baby's napkin, unfold it, lay it across her lap. Take my seat.

Egypt takes the fork full of macaroni and cheese, leans in toward me, places the fork to my lips, I open, eat it with delight, happy as hell she wants and needs to feed her man.

"Thank you, baby."

"You know you're my baby, right, King?" She questions.

"I wouldn't have it any other way."

"This doesn't make any sense."

"Doesn't have to. Everything in life doesn't need an explanation."

"I was thinking that when I was wrecking my brain trying to rationalize the irrational."

"I don't want to waste our precious time trying to apply for some sort of label to place on what we have."

"And what do we have, King?"

"This is love, baby."

"Too soon, no way, I don't even know your middle name. Haven't met your mother yet."

"Tell me you don't love me, Egypt." I demand.

She can't.

I take my fork full of crab cake and place it into Egypt's mouth. I tease her with it, make her lick the fork, slide her tongue out to capture the food.

"You're hungry, right, baby?" I question.

":Yes. Let me have it." she replies.

"How bad do you want it?"

"More than you know, King."

"Promise me you'll waste no more time trying to figure this thing out."

"I promise."

"I do have a question, Egypt."

"What is that, baby?"

"Why are you so beautiful?"

"Because I'm a reflection of you, King. Beautiful, black man."

"Talking like that may get you off the market." I smile.

"I'm yours for the taking."

I reach for my phone. Pull it out. "Excuse me, baby." I open the message, type "Need to eat your pussy for dessert, Egypt." I click send. She pulls her phone from her purse.

"Sorry, King. Let me get this then I'll turn my phone off." She checks her phone, smiles, places it back into her purse. Egypt leans in, tells me to "come closer," kisses me on my lips.

A Telephone Call Away

Her...

Lovely evening with that delightful black man. I stare at him as he makes sure I get into my car safely. Cleans the light dusting of snow off my windshield. Makes sure that everything is in order.

"King, really, all is well. I'm okay, baby. Thank you for dinner."

He leans in to give me a kiss on the lips. Lets me have just a sampling of his tongue. Gives it to me, just a small amount and I want more, already. I lick my lips once he takes that heavenly goodness away from me.

"More where that came from when you're ready, Egypt."

"Okay, baby."

"Drive safe, baby."

"I will."

I watch him through my rearview mirror as he walks to his car. Mmmmm, mmmmm, mmmm, what a walking peace of mind, tall drink of cognac, coated in chocolate that wonderful man is. If I weren't such a lady, I would have invited him home where he'd have the pleasure of witnessing me on all fours sucking his dick long and slow and becoming familiar with every inch of him. Too bad I'm such a fucking lady. Now, I get to go home with a wet ass.

Old school R&B reverberates throughout my truck and sets the tone to the wonderfully horny mood I'm in. There's something so exotic and scary and pleasant and addicting to what King and I are experiencing right now. Barely knowing one another, yet, knowing one another well enough to embrace and kiss and flirt and drink and text and love one another in private and in a public setting. Affairs of the heart can never be explained and only make sense to the people involved. Never have I seen or experienced something so grand in my life.

As I drive, I think about the precious moment we shared. The thought of him kissing me there. My leg begins to twitch. Seems like he knows all of my secrets. How can he touch me just one time and make me his? He makes the rain fall down on me. Can't concentrate when I think of him. Can hardly breathe for the trembling in my thighs. Breathe easy.

My phone rings. I'm hesitant to answer. I prefer to allow my panties to get soaked and want nothing to get in the way of my night time drive home with thoughts of King on my mind... and him kissing me there, and there, and there.

I answer through my steering wheel button. Technology is great with hands-free calling.

"Hello."

"Hey, baby." King says.

"King? What are you doing?"

"Checking on my baby."

"You're so sweet." I admit as I blush.

"You're sweeter. Like dessert."

"Is that right?" I question.

"Yes, Egypt. Speaking of which, when do I get my dessert?"

I blush. Pussy throbs at an all time high. Swallow hard. Licks lips. Exhales.

"Soon, baby."

"I want to eat your pussy now, Egypt."

"Not now, King. Too soon."

"Egypt."

"King, please, you're messing up my concentration."

"Why?"

"Because..."

"Why, Egypt. Tell me those thoughts you've been keeping from me."

"I...I...I'm not keeping..."

"You're lying."

Silence.

"King, please..."

"Egypt, tell me you don't want me to taste you."

"King..."

"You couldn't tell me that you don't love me. Now you can't tell me that you don't want me to slide my tongue in that pretty pussy. Can you?"

"King, this is not right."

"It's so right. The thought of having your pussy splash in my face is right. And, you know it."

"King. I gotta get home."

"Egypt. Let me come over and slide this hot tongue in that wet pussy."

Hard swallows.

"Is it wet, Egypt?"

Silence.

"Egypt, is that sweet pussy wet for me, baby? Don't fucking lie to me."

"Yes! It's wet, King. You happy now?"

"No, I'm not happy."

"Why? I just told you it was wet." I'm fucking with him now.

"I want my face between your thighs. I want to taste my pussy. I want you to come in my mouth. I want your juices on my lips. Now. Tonight." King demands.

"Not tonight, King."

"Tonight, Egypt. Tell me you don't want me. You can't."

"I can't tell you that. I do want you, King."

"Tell me what you want, Egypt."

"I want you. All of you." I confess.

"You want me to taste it, suck it, fuck it, empty myself inside of it...damn, baby, please. Let me please you." He pleads.

"King, please, I'm almost home. Let me call you later."

"No. Stay on the phone with me. Is your pussy wet?"

"Yes." I'm embarrassed to admit.

"Nipples hard?" He questions with excitement in his voice.

"Yes, God, yes, they're hard." I tell him as the tension mounts.

"You want my tongue on you, don't you?" King asks.

"Yes."

"Tell me how bad."

"So fucking bad." I say with an urgency to have his tongue planted inside of me.

"Tell me again, Egypt."

"I want you so fucking bad right now, King."

"I'm coming over. Unlock the door. Get that pussy ready

for me."

"King, we don't even know one another."

The Original Sin

Him...

"Egypt..."

"King..."

"Open the door, Egypt."

"You followed me home, King?"

"Baby, couldn't help myself."

"The door is unlocked."

"Good."

I walk up the stairs to her townhouse. Landscaping on either side of the staircase, nice driveway, beautiful community, and I don't give a damn about none of this shit right now. She can take me on a tour after we wake up in each other's arms tomorrow. Reaching the burgundy steel door, with the glass window, I look through it and can see Egypt's silhouette. I push the door open, gently close it behind me, lock it.

"Put the alarm on."

She obliges. Walking over to the door, she reaches up to the keypad, puts the house alarm on. Turns around, faces me. I can see terror in her eyes. Her spirit is full of lust. The smell of her flesh getting hot fuels my desire and rage and love and lust for her.

"We will learn in the process. Please baby. I need to taste you. Need to get next to you. Now. Tonight."

"King...this doesn't make any sense. This is not how this is supposed to go."

"Do you love me, Egypt?"

She hesitates, walks away. Takes her coat off. She's heated. Mad, happy, confused, attracted, she's delirious, I can see it in her eyes. Her coat falls to the floor. She's walking like there's a flood, like rain and hail and wind and a tornado are between her legs, in that nasty, wet, delicious cave that belongs to me.

I walk up behind her. Her body trembles. She grabs the edge of the burnt orange sofa. I pull her body to me. I know she can feel me, feel this staff, this rod, its harder than the Rock of Gibraltar, has her name written all over it, etched in eternity, its hers and she doesn't even know it.

"Egypt. I know you love me. Because I fucking love you." I kiss the back of her neck. Her body melts in my arms. I kiss it once more. Make my way to the back of her ear, I kiss and suck the lobe, whisper in her ear, "I love you. I've loved you. I fucking love you. You get that?" Pulling her closer to me, I press my length against her ass. Grabbing her waist, my hand travels to her breasts, I gently run my fingertips over her nipples. They're at attention, needing and wanting my attention.

"Take your shirt off, Egypt."

I turn her around, watch her as she removes the garment that's in the way of me and my Tootsie-Roll nipples. I walk up to her, press her back against the wall, remove her bra.

"King..." She's too weak to fight the feeling. I'm just a step above her, as all I want to do is spend the rest of my life with her. I get exhausted thinking about the possibilities.

Kissing her forehead, kissing her nose, her cheek, she grabs me, pulls me into a passionate kiss. Gives me her tongue. Ooooh, it's so wet and hot and juicy and nasty and perfect; it's mine, all mine. I suck it. I love it. We lick one another's tongues until they land in the other's mouth. She lets out a sultry moan.

"King, baby," she pleads.

My sex drive is one hundred miles and running. My heated gaze reveals all of my freakish thoughts. The way she's responding to my touch lets me know she can go all fucking night. The temperature in my heart is rising to a boiling point.

"Touch me, Egypt."

She reaches out her hand, I step back. She reaches again, I pull away. Her full breasts are bouncing, nipples at an all time high, they've reached their peak. She walks toward me, as I unbutton my top. "Come and get me, Egypt." She moves closer to me, like a feline, she's in heat, serious heat, nothing makes sense in her mind, she's got that glazed look over her eyes and face, my pretty pussycat is in heat. She's making serious love to me already with those piercing, almond-shaped, honey-coated eyes. This erotic game of cat and mouse has me ready to explode.

My chest is exposed, she reaches for it. I allow her to touch it. Taking her finger, she places it into her mouth, gets it nice and wet and caresses my nipple with it.

"Suck it, baby. It's yours," I command her.

Moving in closer, she greets the center of my chest with her award-winning, luscious lips. She takes my nipple into her mouth, slowly licks and sucks on it, making it her own, marking her territory, branding me with her lovely goodness. Naughty cat is etching her name into my flesh. She's letting me know that this is hers.

"Good girl. Hold me, Egypt." Gently, yet deliberately she unzips my denims. I take my shirt off, toss it to the floor. She sees what I have in store for her and I witness the pleasure in her eyes. I'm ready for her to see all the nasty fuck faces I'm going to try to contain as she gives me what I already know will be a pussy so damn good, I won't be able to contain myself.

She takes me into her hand, my pants drop to the floor. I step out of them. She bends down to kiss it, but I stop her. Placing my hand on her chin, I kiss her lips and say, "My middle name is Dionne." She smiles. Bends down to taste the chocolate candy bar she's been craving for so long. I stop her. She her sweet lips again. "My mother makes a great sweet potato pie. She already knows about you." She smiles. Her breathing is tempered, staggered. I pull her into an embrace.

My tongue lets loose, aims right for the full, bountiful, beautiful breasts. I love them, lick them, and my tongue traces the nipple. I place them together with my hands and she lets out a moan that makes fluid leak from my staff. Sucking them with a vengeance, I take my right hand and unbutton her pants. She helps me. They fall to the floor. She steps out of them.

We move together toward the flight of stairs. She leads the way. My lioness prepares to take me to her den. Unlike Daniel, there's no harm awaiting me there, only pleasure, and satisfaction. I pull her back towards me, give her my tongue once again, she's so anxious, her kisses are choppy, hot, excited, she's ready. I tell her, "I know your Dad's name is Joe. You have two sisters. You're the baby of the family. You're five-eleven. I love everything about you."

She walks up the flight of stairs and the view of her oversized butterscotch ass swaying in front of me is more than I can witness at this moment. Stopping Egypt in her tracks, I bend her open, taking my hands and spreading her legs, I plant my face at the center of her goodness. Sweet surrender... her walls are set ablaze by my tongue. Deep tongue fucking into her pretty pink hole excites me just as much as she is delighted. Her ass bounces onto my face and I bite it, grab it, smack it, to give her a sting to keep the juices flowing. I don't neglect her sweet snatch for too long and make my way back there.

"KING!" she yells. Her voice quivers with heavenly goodness. I can hear angels singing all around us. She's right where I want her to be. Her seductive moans and cries for mercy are as out of sync and fast and breathtaking as the rapid throbbing inside her sugar coated walls.

"BABY!" she screams. "I need it now, King. Please, let's go to the bedroom." She pulls away from me, almost running up the flight stairs. I watch as she heads toward the pleasure palace where pleasing that pretty pussy will be my only purpose in life.

She waits for me at the bedroom door. Excitement and that glazed look of erotic euphoria covers her, like a fog, she's immersed in weakness of the flesh. I walk up to her. Kiss her shoulder. Bite her lips. She takes my hand in hers, pulls me in a frantic, rushed state. We make our way to her bed. Big, king sized soft, pillow top heavenly bed built for a queen. The smell of fresh linens mixed with the scent of my baby makes me feel like I'm at home.

Egypt lies on her back. She doesn't hesitate to spread that pussy real nasty for me. Tells me, "I was born in Newark.

1972. Been watching you for a year or more. Been loving you at least that long." I smile. Laying on top of her, her soft, fluffy, buttery-soft skin sizzles when I greet it.

I moan as I feel her breasts against my chest. Egypt pulls me into a sensational kiss. Begs for me to love her hard, then soft, then deep. I oblige.

She yelled and cooed, "Oooooh," as the peak of me rushed into her wetness, her dampness, drowned me so good. Her heat and softness moves so deliciously with my fire and rock-hardness.

"Good pussy, baby," I manage to get those words out. Finding a good rhythm is hard, she's so god-damn good, and soft and sweet and damn, I love her. I pull out, then rush back in like my life depends on it, over and over and over again.

Her purrs of satisfaction lets me know that I'm getting the job done. Her nails make new pathways into my back, and the pleasurable pain in welcomed as it represents battle scars on this battlefield of love. Like we're making love after war. Like I'm trying to get this right. Oh baby, I'm gonna make it right.

She pulls me in deeper into her steamy wet cave. Controls the tempo of my thrusts by grabbing my ass, she guides me, doesn't say a word, I know who's boss. Whew, she's a greedy lover. Won't let me control my pace.

"You're going to make me come too soon, Egypt," I beg.

I manage to free myself from my greedy baby's grip. Pulling out, she almost has tears in her eyes. I need a few moments to recover, to slow this down, to shift my focus. My excitement is going to make round one end in record time. I need to cherish every last drip drop of this bountiful love-making.

She reaches for me. Her nipples, perky, speaking to me, begging for my complete, and undivided attention. I look at her pussy. It's wet, begging for the same affection her breasts are. Her lips, they need me too. She calls out for me, "King, please. More, baby. Now."

The word "Now," when I used it had a different connotation, it was urgent and needing and longing, but when you're on the other end of it, its scary, its demanding, its pressure, its heat and lust and love, and it all collides, all on a collision course of passion.

I oblige.

Taking my shaft into my hands, the chocolate rod shines from my baby's desire for me. I give it to her again, pull it out, tell her "Look at what you've done to me." I bite my lips. Reach down, lick her breasts. Kiss her. Lick her. I pull out again. She cries, "King, please."

I tell her, "Look at how wet you got me." I thrust harder inside of her. About to lose my mind. In and out, out and in, my strokes are full of force, of rage, I hear her cries, I feel my blood boiling, I suck her breasts.

"King!" she screams. She raises her hips. Howls as I enter her over and over again. I look down, see her glistening, tell her "Baby, look what you're doing to me." She looks, she yells, "KING! I'm going to come. Ooooooh, you're gonna make me come all over you."

Midnight grinding, heart rates climbing. She's giving me every ounce of her love like she somehow owes it to me.

We're fucking.

Fucking.

Making love.

Loving, like two souls that have loved in this, past and concurrent lifetimes.

We're loving, sexing, fucking, like animals born to breed.

Fucking, like we're trying to capture air we need to

breathe.

"Make me come, King." She demands. I pull out. Too much. Forcefully, my face lands in between her tenderness and my tongue dances a jig with her clit. She's screaming, crying, begging, in ecstasy, she's nuts, out of control.

"King, I need it now." Egypt grabs me, pulls me back on top of her.

"Give me my dick, King," she orders.

"This is the best pussy I've ever had. You know that, right?"

"Give me that come, King." She demands. What a beautiful, thirsty, heaven-sent wench she is. She's blowing my mind; fucking me like this, like she wants me to love her.

"I wanna give you this come, Egypt," I struggle. Look down at how her pussy receives me. Shit. I can't figure this out. So tight. So wet. She's fucking with me, giving me this pussy like this.

"Fuck me like you love me, King." She insists.

"Is this sweet, wet pussy all mine, baby?"

"Yes, God, yes, all yours, King." She hollers. Gives me her tongue. Her tongue resuscitates my soul and lulls me to a place of satisfaction I have not visited in a very long time.

"Good girl." I whisper in her ear.

Sliding into her with all I have, she cries, I cry, we both cry in unison. I feel her holy ocean rain down on me and its too much to bear.

I had been invited into the room that makes the rain.

As I delve deeper inside of her, I brush the tears away from her glorious face. I kiss her tears, shed my own.

Have Mercy

Her...

He bites my neck, whispers in my ear, "You're so good, Egypt, I love everything about you."

Once again releasing, I dig deep into King's back as I softly yell in gratification, "King."

He moves away from me and I'm momentarily paralyzed.

"King...No," I whisper as he caresses my leg with his hand.

Grabbing my feet, my left lay in his right hand and he grabs my right with his left. He towers over me, and I'm anxious as to what he has planned. But I'm feeling desperate, wanting him to enter me once again.

"King," I softly yell. He spreads my legs far and wide. My big toes enter his mouth alternately. He spreads my legs further apart.

"King...I can't take this. Fuck me, please." I cry.

"You're so greedy, Egypt." A devilish smirk covers his face.

As the tip of his rod bounces against the surface of my love, I swallow hard, my nipples harden even more. Unable to break free, King continues to lick my toes, one by one this time, my legs – spread so far apart. His dick, teasing me as it glides across my clit – it's knocking at my door.

"Grab the headboard, Egypt." He commands and I reach back, my arms above my head, hold on as he instructed. I look at him – my feet still in his hands, my legs still far and wide. His length, still taunting me.

"King. Baby, please."

As my toe leaves his mouth, he asks me, "Do you like it?"

"I love it King. Please..."

"You made me wait so long for this good loving, Egypt. Damn it."

In a rush, his head travels down my thighs and quickly lands on my righteousness, he licks it, full, wide, kisses it once more, makes his way back up to my toes, both of my legs still wide apart.

"King," I beg.

"Close your eyes."

My eyes slowly shut and he moves my legs further apart. His dick moves in circles across the surface – gently, yet deliberately. He's marking his territory. Branding the word KING into my love, embedding this moment in my memory. Showing me who the boss is, the conqueror, the master of my domain.

His dick bounces against my clit, then he gives me the tip quickly.

"Please, don't do this to me." I beg.

"You want it, Egypt?"

"Yes..."

"Take it."

I open my eyes and reach for him – his rod. I reach.

"Close your eyes. Picture me, King."

I reach again. He pulls away.

"No hands. Take it."

"King, please, just give it to me."

"Take it. Let me watch you take this dick baby."

Eyes closed, heart beating fast, hands on headboard, I motion my body to take what is mine. My hips roll frantically, as his length touches my walls. I can't get it. I roll harder, faster, reaching up, my legs shake.

"King! Please, fuck me!" I softly yell as his tip glides across my clit.

"Take it, Egypt. You look so good."

"King, give it to me, or you'll never get close enough to smell it again."

I roll my hips with everything I have in me, trying to capture it.

"You're spoiled, baby."

He plays with me more. I can't move. I reach for him.

"No hands."

"King, you give me that dick, now, or..."

"Hush," he yells softly in my ear as he rams deep into me.

Lord, have mercy.

The Morning After

Her...

Feels like a thousand sunrises and sunsets had gone by, and yet, that still wasn't enough time with King. I watch him as he sleeps. He turns over, opens his eyes. He smiles. Tells me, "Go into my jacket pocket. There's a small, red box in there for you. White bow."

Like a kid on Christmas day, I rush to retrieve the surprise. Climb back into the bed. I smile. Look at my King. I say, "Baby, what's this?"

"Something I got for you about six months ago."

"Baby, we didn't know each other six months ago."

"Yes we did. We've been speaking to one another for over a year, through our words, at "Nights.""

I open the box. He looks with excitement in his eyes.

"Oh My God..."

literary field. Her debut novel, Mistress Memoirs allowed her to be the recipient of the 2009 AALA for Break Out Author of the year; and her sophomore novel, Ask Nicely and I Might was the 2011 AALA winner for Mystery of the year. She has adopted the motto of "Why Blend in when you are born to stand out" and is always striving to absorb and digest all that life has to offer, while finding new ways to connect with the world through good story telling. Visit Lorraine at www.lorraineelzia.com.

LaLaina Knowles

LaLaina Knowles is a contemporary writer who has made her mark in the industry as one of the hottest voices in African American literature. She has written and published several books such as A Wife of Abraham, Twisted Karma, and Chocolat Historie D'Amour (contributing author). When LaLaina is not working on her next literary project, she manages her life coaching consulting firm where she is also employed as a Certified Life Strategies Coach Practitioner; she also spends quality time with her daughters, volunteers with at-risk youth, and advocate for the rights of foster children across the United States. In addition, LaLaina serves as an advocate for Reading Is Fundamental, is Co-Founder and Vice President of Moving on up Ministries based in Plant City, FL., is an active member of the Girls Scouts of America and volunteers at the Department of Juvenile Justice. LaLaina attended Georgia Southern University in Statesboro, Georgia where she majored in Early Childhood Education and is currently working towards her goal of obtaining her Doctorate of Psychology emphasizing in Clinical Psychology. Her life's philosophy entails focusing on inspiring every person she comes in contact with and possessing and maintaining a spirit of humbleness and gratitude; she works diligently daily to make a difference in the world and the lives of others. LaLaina currently resides in Central Florida with her daughters. For more information about LaLaina Knowles please visit: www. ladyellepublishing.com or www.lalainaknowles.com

Ebonee Monique

Ebonee Monique graduated from Florida A&M University with a Bachelor of Science degree in Public Relations. She was nominated as Breakout Author of the Year for African American Literary Award Show in 2009 for her debut novel "Suicide Diaries". Prior to becoming a published author, Ebonee Monique served as Morning Show Host and Operations Manager for WANM 90.5FM in Tallahassee, Florida and produced an on-air weekly entertainment segment on TOUCH 106.1FM in Boston, MA. She currently lives in the state of Florida.

www.eboneemonique.com

Elissa Gabrielle

The sky is the limit for this sassy, sundry and prolific author. Elissa Gabrielle has broken the ceiling of literary excellence with her gift in the skill of multi-genre writing. The author of two poetry books, four novels and contributor to multiple anthologies, Elissa has proven herself to be well-versed in artistic creativity.

Her colloquial and imaginative creations have lead to sensual and seductive inclusions in Zane's Purple Panties, Erogenous Zone: A Sexual Voyage, Mocha Chocolate: A Taste of Ecstasy, and more.

As a Literary Entrepreneur, Elissa is the founder of the greeting card line, Greetings from the Soul: The Elissa Gabrielle Collection, collaborator and creator of The Triumph of My Soul, and publisher of Peace In The Storm Publishing. Elissa has managed to turn relatively unknown authors into household names and has molded and shaped the careers of some of today's brightest literary stars. In addition to these innovative achievements, Elissa has graced the covers of Conversations Magazine, Big Time Publishing Magazine, Disilgold Soul Magazine and has been featured in Urbania

Magazine and Black Literature Magazine.

Peace In The Storm Publishing has been nominated in several categories in the African American Literary Awards Show, and has won Independent Publisher of the Year in 2009, 2010 and 2011. In addition, Elissa Gabrielle won for Self-Published Author of the Year in 2010 for her explosive novel, "A Whisper to a Scream."

From the novelty of her writing, to her highly-regarded greeting card line and the successful culmination of her publishing company; Elissa Gabrielle remains an ingenious and creative force to be reckoned with in terms of delivering distinct, fulfilling and entertaining literature. By pushing herself to stay a cut above the rest, Elissa Gabrielle brilliantly and consistently delivers Literary best.

www.peaceinthestormpublishing.com

CPSIA information can be obtained at www.ICGtesting.com
Printed in the USA
LVOW041149130512

281510LV00002B/63/P

9 780985 076313